Ms. Lorraine Madden
315 Lake Bluff Ct
Orange Park, FL 32073-2890

D0464239

PRAISE FOR

The Cross Gardener

"Sharp prose, clever characterizations, thought-provoking insights . . . fresh and spiritual."

—Don Piper, *New York Times* bestselling author
of *90 Minutes in Heaven* and *Heaven Is Real*

"Passionate, spiritual, and thought-provoking . . . [A] beautifully written book."

—Glenn Beck, talk radio and FOX news host,
#1 *New York Times* bestselling author

"Celebrates the incredible joys of the human experience."

—Kevin Milne, author of *The Nine Lessons*

"Fans of author Jason F. Wright's previous inspirational novels . . . will delight in this uplifting tale."   —*Birmingham Magazine*

"Jason Wright's storytelling captures the reader's heart and draws them along on the journey to find forgiveness, acceptance, and peace through this loving tale."   —*Wichita Falls Times Record News*

"*The Cross Gardener* is a quiet book with a quiet message of hope . . . Wright is to be commended for his passion and commitment to his subject."   —*Deseret News*

"Plenty of uplift and tradition-affirming sentiment."

—*Publishers Weekly*

Berkley titles by Jason F. Wright

THE WEDNESDAY LETTERS
THE CROSS GARDENER
THE SEVENTEEN SECOND MIRACLE

The Seventeen Second Miracle

· A NOVEL ·

JASON F. WRIGHT

BERKLEY BOOKS, NEW YORK

THE BERKLEY PUBLISHING GROUP
Published by the Penguin Group
Penguin Group (USA) Inc.
375 Hudson Street, New York, New York 10014, USA
Penguin Group (Canada), 90 Eglinton Avenue East, Suite 700, Toronto, Ontario M4P 2Y3, Canada
(a division of Pearson Penguin Canada Inc.)
Penguin Books Ltd., 80 Strand, London WC2R 0RL, England
Penguin Group Ireland, 25 St. Stephen's Green, Dublin 2, Ireland (a division of Penguin Books Ltd.)
Penguin Group (Australia), 250 Camberwell Road, Camberwell, Victoria 3124, Australia
(a division of Pearson Australia Group Pty. Ltd.)
Penguin Books India Pvt. Ltd., 11 Community Centre, Panchsheel Park, New Delhi—110 017, India
Penguin Group (NZ), 67 Apollo Drive, Rosedale, North Shore 0632, New Zealand
(a division of Pearson New Zealand Ltd.)
Penguin Books (South Africa) (Pty.) Ltd., 24 Sturdee Avenue, Rosebank, Johannesburg 2196,
South Africa

Penguin Books Ltd., Registered Offices: 80 Strand, London WC2R 0RL, England

This book is an original publication of The Berkley Publishing Group.

This is a work of fiction. Names, characters, places, and incidents either are the product of the author's imagination or are used fictitiously, and any resemblance to actual persons, living or dead, business establishments, events, or locales is entirely coincidental. The publisher does not have any control over and does not assume any responsibility for author or third-party websites or their content.

ISBN 978-1-61664-924-1

PRINTED IN THE UNITED STATES OF AMERICA

To the teachers who believed.

ACKNOWLEDGMENTS

As always, my thanks begin with my wife and biggest fan, Kodi. She performs more Seventeen Second Miracles in a day than anyone I've ever known. Gratitude galore is also due my parents, my siblings, their spouses, and their children. *(Except for the ones who don't like me. You know who you are.)*

A big shout-out to my inaugural editor-for-a-day, Chris Dalton, who read and expertly edited this manuscript in a minivan amid flying Happy Meal toys and broken animal crackers during an 1,800-mile road trip with his wife, Penny, and two young children. Now, *that's* dedication!

Fist bumps to the usual suspects in my professional corner: Sandy Harding, Leslie Gelbman, Susan Allison, Laurie Liss, and the fantastic publicists and sales reps that helped you discover this book today.

Literary hugs to my kitchen cabinet of early readers and critics: Matt "B+" Birch, Cherie "Grace" Call, Michelle "Mission Mom" Denson, Stuart "Little" and Katie "Helga" Freakley, Jessica "NASCAR" Garman, Angie "Sprite" Godfrey, Kevin "Redonkulously Talented"

Milne, Laurie "Coasters" Paisley, Kelly "Midge" Phillips, Heidi "Victoria" Taylor, Beth "Eat at Joe's" Wobbe.

Finally, to the thousands of book clubs around the country: Thank you for embracing me, my books, and their messages. If you'd like to invite me to visit your book club in person or by phone, please visit my website at www.jasonfwright.com and make a request today. *(Yes, I can be bribed with baked goods.)*

1970

RₑX CONNER FELL IN LOVE WITH A BODY OF WATER.

The popular lake was part of Chris Greene Park, located in Albemarle County, Virginia, just a few minutes from Charlottesville's northern city limits.

By the summer of 1970, the teen was also in love with his new job, employed by the county's Parks & Recreation Department as a lifeguard.

But mostly, he loved a girl.

The young brunette had thick, long hair that made her easy to spot from his wooden perch overlooking the lake's sandy man-made beach.

Rex spotted her often.

They met after his shift on July Fourth as Rex played Frisbee with friends in a field by the water.

The brunette made trips with her mother to and from their station wagon carrying picnic supplies. When she made the first trip alone, Rex accidentally launched the Frisbee in her direction.

The girl introduced herself, and after a few minutes of awkward small talk, Rex looked her in the eyes and asked permission to give her a nickname. He'd given nearly everyone he knew a nickname.

"I guess," she said, gathering and tucking a lock of hair behind her ear.

"Sparks."

She laughed. "Sparks?"

"Sparks. Because that's what I see all around you."

She blushed, just as he knew she would, and that was the beginning of the summer that changed Rex Conner.

REX ANGLED WITH HIS BOSS TO WORK THE DAYS SHE PROMised she would be coming to the lake. Which, given their budding romance, was often.

Though far from a seasoned lifeguard, he'd learned the first rule: Keep your eyes on the water.

Sometimes Rex watched Sparks swim alone in the deeper water, back and forth between two orange buoys. She was, at least in his eyes, an expert in every stroke. He particularly enjoyed watching her towel off standing back onshore. She would carefully remove her bulky swim cap and shake her head back and forth, breathing life back into her matted, tangled hair.

He saw sparks then, too.

Sometimes watching the water meant he could watch Sparks

play with her younger sister. The two squeaked and danced in the shallow waves like SeaWorld dolphins. Their mother would sneak up and take pictures, then race off screaming in delight as her daughters chased and kicked water at her.

The younger sister was a wiry eight-year-old with light brown hair—shorter than her sister's but styled the same—and a laugh you could hear from nearly every shallow corner of Chris Greene Lake.

Rex gave his pint-sized friend a nickname, too. He chose "Flick," because she was just like her older sister, but smaller and full of potential to light the world on fire. He promised her that someday she'd sparkle just like her older sister.

Sparks's sister flickered and beamed every time he called her by the new name.

By the end of the summer, even Flick's mother had adopted the moniker.

The relationship between Rex and Sparks became a classic summertime romance.

Rex ate Sunday dinners with her family. He went with them on a sightseeing day trip to Williamsburg and, later, one to the Shenandoah Valley. They invited him to family game night, picnics, church, and even a church picnic.

When Rex wasn't working at the lake, he was pulled to Sparks's side, stuck between love and lust and feeling like an older, more mature soul trapped in the body of a sixteen-year-old.

More often than not, Flick was right there at his other side.

Rex enjoyed watching the two girls interact. Not simply sisters, they were friends—best friends, despite the age difference. Seeing them together made him wish he weren't an only child.

When Sparks took a break from the lake water to soak in the sun on a beach towel, Flick followed.

When Sparks rolled from her back to her stomach, Flick did the same, even discreetly and awkwardly adjusting her swimsuit in the same way.

When Sparks stood, stretched, and returned to the water to cool off and show off for her lifeguard boyfriend, Flick followed.

While swimming, Sparks often arched her back and leaned backward into the water to remove the hair from her forehead and face. She held her nose as she lifted her head slowly out, face toward the sky, thick hair streaking behind her and clinging to her shoulders and the back of her swimsuit. Then she looked at Rex in his tall wooden lifeguard chair to see if he'd been watching.

Of course he had.

So Flick did the same, awkwardly dipping her head backward and choking on dirty lake water as she surfaced. Then she also looked over at Rex.

He would laugh and blow her a kiss.

Flick giggled and covered her cheeks, so Sparks caught the kisses instead.

Usually, when Sparks took out her sketch pad at a picnic table to practice her charcoal drawings, Flick would sit across from her and color on sheets borrowed from her big sister. Many of the drawings read "For Rex" in one of the corners.

Rex's favorite creation was a crayon drawing of a boy in a red swimsuit overlooking a deep blue oval lake filled with round, fat fish with bubble eyes and smiley faces. The boy had a crown and oversized eyes, and sat high in a throne that looked more like a tower than a lifeguard's chair. A sun with thick rays shined from the left corner of the paper. A few pillowy clouds sat to the right. There were no swimmers in the lake, just a stick figure lifeguard with spiky hair and bumpy muscles watching over the water with wide, attentive eyes and a grin.

WHENEVER REX REMINISCED ABOUT HIS SUMMER WITH Sparks and Flick, which he had so often through the years that the details never blurred, he found time to praise the girls' mother. Worried that her daughter and Rex would make a mistake that would haunt them and effectively end their adolescence, Flick was often sent to accompany the two hormone-crazed teens.

Neither seemed to mind. The threesome saw movies on the downtown mall, ate pizza on the famed Corner by UVA's campus, played volleyball at the lake, and walked the heavily wooded trails. It was on those walks that Flick most often appeared at the most inopportune times.

"Wait up, guys!" Flick said, running toward them as they disappeared into the woods. "Mom said I could come."

"Oh she did, did she? Well, I don't know about that," her older sister said.

"Uh-huh. She did. She said she didn't want you to get lost."

Rex would smile and tickle Flick under the neck with his fingertips. "What if *you* get lost?" he said, and he and his sweetheart would race ahead, around a corner, and out of view.

Flick followed, racing and hollering, "Hey! Wait up! Hey, guys!"

But they were never far ahead. The couple snuck into the trees, shared a few clumsy but passionate wet kisses, and then jumped out onto the trail when Flick approached.

"Gotcha!" Rex teased, and Flick breathed easy.

"Stop it. Mom said if you lost me out here, I'd be in big, big trouble. And so would you."

Sparks hugged her little sister. "We'd never lose you, Flick. Never."

Then, like many times before, and a few times after, they raced back to their mother.

Every single day that summer, Rex felt as if he were one step closer to being a man.

He was almost right.

He was just seventeen seconds from growing up.

REX JOKED THAT VIRTUALLY EVERYONE WHO SWAM AT CHRIS Greene that summer knew that Flick's birthday fell on Labor Day. She'd convinced her parents to throw a huge party at the lake and, naturally, Rex was invited as a guest. Flick clapped and jumped twice in the air when Rex said he would be honored and that he wasn't scheduled to work that day. He'd worked the Fourth of July and his supervisor at Parks & Recreation said he shouldn't have to work both holidays.

Still, Rex knew his invitation to the party wasn't just for fun. Sparks's mother wanted another set of trained eyes for the gaggle of girls who would be running in and out of the water, playing games, doing what kids do best at birthday parties.

The afternoon was filled with pizza, cake, silly hats, balloons, plastic cups of root beer, and gifts. The gifts sat stacked high in a pyramid on a picnic table near the food. Flick wanted to open them last.

For many years after, Rex remembered Flick wanting to save the gifts until the end. Not because it was the most exciting thing about the party or the best part of the day, but because it was the *least* important. What mattered most was having friends there, having family around.

Rex followed that example and taught his son to do the same. "Presents are nice, and who doesn't enjoy unwrapping a gift?" he would say. "But the real gift is your *time*. Your *laughter*. The memories we make *together*." The lesson was old-fashioned and Rex knew it. But it didn't just stay with his son, it may have saved him.

After Flick's birthday lunch and a short nature hike—some of the children at the party had never been to the lake or seen the trails before—Rex and Sparks led the younger kids out to the lake for water games.

Flick's mother stayed behind to watch the gifts and to position herself where she could still easily keep an eye on the girls.

The group played in the shallow water on the lake's man-made beach. They played tic-tac-toe in the sand with their feet.

Rex took a turn playing tag with a plastic water gun. He showed off a little, too, squirting some of his friends and being silly for the two lifeguards on duty, both of them friends from a long summer of working side by side.

At one point Rex began throwing a Frisbee for the kids to catch in the knee-deep water. They took turns diving and splashing, sometimes one at a time, sometimes in a frenzied scrum to see who could emerge with the bright yellow disk.

When Rex tired of the game, he tossed the Frisbee on the water's edge and spotted Sparks twenty yards away. She was arching her back again in the deeper water, gathering her long hair and pulling it into a thick rope against her neck and back.

Rex took his time enjoying the view and snuck up from behind. He covered her eyes. "Guess who?" he said. "Clock's ticking." Then, as the game demanded, Rex began to count. "One, two, three." It wasn't the first time they'd played the game, and Sparks played her part.

"Mitchell Voltron?"

"Four, five, six," Rex continued.

"John Lennon?"

"Seven, eight."

"James Taylor?"

"Nine, ten, eleven, twelve."

"Santana?"

"Faster! Thirteen, fourteen."

"Tina Turner?"

"Hey!" Rex cackled. "Fifteen, sixteen."

"The handsome Rex Conner?"

"Yes! Seventeen seconds! But that's *way* too long." Rex stole a kiss and Sparks instinctively turned to see if her mother had seen.

She hadn't, Sparks reasoned, because her mother was standing near the table with both hands on her forehead, shielding the sun, studying the water, her focus far beyond the young lovers.

Sparks's eyes went to the spot where her sister and the others had been.

Flick was gone.

Rex's eyes went to the deeper water, as he was trained, and easily spotted the yellow Frisbee floating atop the surface, glowing in the darker water like the sun peeking through black rain clouds. But Rex saw more than just the Frisbee; he saw frantic splashing, twin thin arms grabbing and clawing at the water.

"Lifeguard!" he screamed, and he dove forward, slicing through, then knifing through, the surface and swimming freestyle, churning the water fast and violently, his arms and legs fueled by fear and an adrenaline his body had never known.

He reached the child well before the other lifeguard and pulled her to the surface. He put his arm around her, just as the training and practice and manuals had shown, and swam with the other arm, towing her on her back to safety.

A crowd had gathered at the shore.

Sparks and her panicked mother stood like twin statues, stiff, hands over their mouths.

Flick's body was blue and limp.

Rex performed CPR, but his own panic made it impossible to keep proper form and the other lifeguard pushed him out of the way.

They worked on Flick, counting aloud and regurgitating lessons learned as another parent ran to a pay phone to call an ambulance.

Rex backed away from the scene and covered his face.

Sparks trembled and squeezed her mother's hands.

"Lisa!" they shouted together. "Flick!"

Sparks's mother pulled away. She pushed another teenage boy to the side and stood nose to nose with Rex, her face flaming red with rage and confusion. "How could you?"

The other lifeguard took over CPR and the race to save Flick continued.

"How long were you horsing around, Rex?" She breathed and the anger faded to tears. "How long, Rex?"

Tears morphed into deep sobs as she pounded on his bare chest.

Rex answered by covering his face and calling on a God he barely knew.

Just a few feet away, in the shadow of a stack of unopened birthday gifts, Sparks knelt beside her lifeless sister, saying prayers and crying teenage tears of her own.

Flick's mother gathered her breath and slowed the sobs long enough to look Rex in the eyes and say the words he would live with for years: "Rex Conner, you just couldn't keep your hands to yourself, could you?"

She followed those with four words only age and disease could wash away: "You killed my angel."

ONE

The Invitation

2010

Dear Student,

Congratulations! You have been recommended to attend the Discussions on the Seventeen Second Miracle.

Discussions begin Wednesday, November 1, 2010, at 5:30 P.M. Discussions will be held at Paper Gems, a bookstore at 1104 East Main Street in Charlottesville.

Discussions will take place on Mondays, Wednesdays, and Fridays at 5:30 P.M., unless otherwise scheduled, and last approximately one hour.

Our final Discussion will be a mandatory field trip on November 24, the day before Thanksgiving.

Being recommended to attend the Discussions on the Seventeen Second Miracle is an honor. I look forward to meeting you.

Sincerely,
Mr. Cole Conner

P.S. Please bring the enclosed pocket watch to our first Discussion.

TWO

Delivery Day

CHRISTMAS, NEW YEAR'S, EASTER, DELIVERY DAY.

They're each special because all four have their own box of memories with unique tastes, scents, and sights. While each brings me joy, only Delivery Day also brings butterflies.

Delivery Day: a day my father would have loved to celebrate at my side.

Delivery Day: It means I celebrate a private holiday less about the past and more about the daily Seventeen Second Miracles that await each of us.

Of course it also means the Discussions are about to begin in the cozy Reading Corner of Paper Gems, my wife's bookstore. And, naturally, it's also the day my new students get their invitations and a pocket watch.

Three weeks ago on Delivery Day, three teenagers recommended to me by the principal at Albemarle High School in

Charlottesville, Virginia, opened their mailboxes and pulled out an envelope with a handwritten note and a pocket watch.

Like always, the watches came from a dealer in Richmond, Virginia.

The notes came on stationery my wife bought for me at a shop on the historic downtown mall in Charlottesville.

Three weeks ago, none of the new students knew me, at least not personally. I didn't ask, I never do, but perhaps they knew me by reputation. After all, this isn't the first year of the Discussions.

I've been fortunate; I've never had a student refuse to attend. Maybe now and again one of them has required a nudge. Or three. But they always show up—eventually. In time, I will understand more fully, but for now I can only accept that this was the first fall we did not finish the Discussions at Paper Gems.

This year's recommendations came in the school's familiar reusable oversized envelope with the red string tie and lines on the back to declare for whom the contents were meant. But they were always meant for me.

As in years past, enclosed I'd found a photo and a handwritten, informal, one-page profile for each student. No official transcripts, no family history, no standardized test scores. But while the format wasn't unique, this year's recommendations were.

Mr. Buhl, a longtime friend of my family and the second Buhl to be AHS principal, recommended for the first time that I welcome only three students into my informal program. In years past, I'd had as few as four and as many as eight. I was disappointed there weren't more, yes, but accepted that he must have known something I didn't about this year's crop. Did he ever.

The principal recommended Miles Bohn and his sweetheart, Kendra Wilson. I'd never had lovebirds attend the Discussions.

Miles was a starting guard for the varsity basketball team.

Kendra was a cheerleader, because her dad bought her first cheerleading outfit when she was four; president of her senior class, because her father had every jock in school work on her campaign; and president of the Young Democrats, something she actually chose for herself because she genuinely liked politics.

Mr. Buhl also recommended Travis Nielson, a wheelchair-bound sophomore who was new to AHS. I'd never had a physically disabled student recommended for the Discussions, and Travis's invitation meant I would spend two days making sure that Paper Gems was really as accessible as our permits said it was.

Just like every year, on the first day of class none of the students knew why they were selected. And just like every year, neither did I.

The Discussions almost ended a few years ago but were saved by the power of compromise and the counsel of a very wise wife. We used to meet on our porch during summer break, but I'd get so involved that Jade and I had *summer* but no break. It wasn't quite as hard on the students—they only came once a week back then—but they still had to give up some hours at their summer jobs. I was about to give up and find a different way to pass on Dad's legacy when Jade suggested moving the meetings to November and holding them in her store, taking our last field trip just before Thanksgiving.

I've always wondered how long Dad would have hosted the Discussions if he could have. Or would he have even wanted to? Teaching me about his daily Seventeen Second Miracles was natural for him. He called me his *captive audience.* But I sense that sharing the origin, the legacy, and telling the stories of his life to complete strangers would have felt boastful.

Dad spoke of it often in general terms, as a movement, something he was grateful to be a part of. But taking too much responsibility would have certainly appeared prideful to him. Though honestly, I *do* feel pride, a sense of honor that it has fallen to me to promote his legacy.

And though I wasn't yet alive, I hope he knows how those tragic seventeen seconds in 1970 changed me, and every student who has ever sat on my porch or in the Reading Corner of Paper Gems.

THREE

Paper Gems

DAD WAS FOR IT; MOM WAS AGAINST IT.

The city of Charlottesville turned its main business street into a pedestrian mall not long after I was born. They tell me it was the biggest local controversy either of them could remember. By the time I was old enough to recall, the quarreling—at home and in town—was over. The downtown mall became the civic center of the city. Paved with bricks and punctuated by trees that seemed to burst through them, the mall is a beautiful, comfortable place.

It is busiest when the weather is warm. In the summer, you'll see people having coffee at 7:00 A.M. and others coming out of the Paramount Theater at midnight. Things slow down a bit beginning in October, but a wonderful thing happens between November and January. The Christmas season brings shoppers looking for the unique gifts found in the galleries and boutiques. New Year's Eve brings thousands of very warmly dressed revelers to celebrate First Night Virginia, a tradition in this town dating back to my own childhood.

What I've liked most since Mom held one of my mittens and Dad the other, is the magical place the mall becomes when the Christmas lights turn on. This happens on the first Saturday in November. Thousands of white lights float in space once the limbs they're on fade in the darkness. It's like the night sky comes down to visit.

On the very end of the mall, just before pedestrians and rich red bricks give way to cars and asphalt, is a bookstore called Paper Gems. It's housed in the ground floor of a building that started out as a dry goods store back when horse-drawn streetcars ran up and down East Main. The store is all Jade's, except for three times a week when I use a section in the back lovingly known as the Reading Corner. It is typically furnished with a white wicker chair, various stools, a big lumpy sofa, and an ugly love seat. But when the Discussions take place, the corner looks like the North Pole.

From the wreaths on the double-entry doors to the window displays that would be at home on Fifth Avenue in New York City, she turns Paper Gems into a Christmas picture book. The Reading Corner gets a big red velvet wingback chair for Santa Claus, a small plastic sleigh, and eight plywood reindeer. Rudolph suffered a fatal encounter with a book cart in 2007 and, in emergency hot-glue-gun surgery, we transplanted his nose onto Blitzen. All of it blends together to convince me that Paper Gems during the holidays helps the message of the Seventeen Second Miracles sink in a little deeper.

I always hope my students feel it, too.

FOUR

Miles and Kendra

I WAS NOT SURPRISED THAT MILES AND KENDRA WERE THE first to arrive.

They walked up holding hands; Kendra waited for him to open the door for her. It was 5:15 P.M.

I greeted them near the cash register. "You're early."

Kendra bounded toward me in a plaid cheerleading skirt and white top visible through her unbuttoned jacket. Her right hand was outstretched and her left dragging Miles through the front of the store. "Hi, Mr. Conner. I'm Kendra Wilson."

"It's a pleasure to meet you. Come on back."

I led them down the center aisle of Paper Gems. Kendra said, "I love this place. It smells like a bookstore should smell. Not like the one at the mall." She closed her eyes and took in another breath. "And it smells like Christmas."

"Thank you, Kendra. Mrs. Conner—Jade—doesn't miss a single detail."

Once the narrow space between bookshelves gave way to the open space of the reading area, I stuck out my hand toward Miles. "And you must be Miles."

"Yeppers." He shook my hand without looking at me. He was already deciding where to sit. He wore faded jeans with thread hanging from a gaping hole in the left knee, a grey T-shirt, and a red-and-blue AHS letterman's jacket.

"Good to meet you, too, Miles. Have a seat."

The couple, still hand in hand, walked toward the love seat that I'd bet Jade they would sit in. But just before they sat, Kendra twirled around and pulled two pocket watches from her Vera Bradley purse. "Are we supposed to give these to you now?"

"Hang on to them, Kendra. We'll talk about that when everyone gets here."

She took a seat by Miles and he immediately flung his left arm around her.

"So what's the ups, Mr. C.," Miles started. "What did we do?"

Kendra slapped his thigh. "Stop."

I grinned. "You didn't do anything. Well, as far as I know. I didn't recommend you, Principal Buhl did."

"I knew it!" Kendra said. "I knew it was tied to school somehow."

"Do we get credit for this?" Miles said.

"Not necessarily on paper, no. But you'll get credit where it counts." I could tell Miles wasn't satisfied, but Kendra drove us on.

"How do you know Principal Buhl?" she said.

"His father and my father were friends for many, many years.

Their friendship began long before you and Miles roamed the halls. Long before I roamed the halls, for that matter."

"So what did PB say I did?" Miles said.

I studied him a moment. "Do you think you're in trouble for something, Miles? You think that's why you were recommended for my program?"

"You tell me."

"You're not in trouble, Mr. Bohn. Being here is a privilege."

Kendra squeezed his hand. "I told you so, Miles." She looked back at me. "What are we discussing? The letter really didn't say. Is anyone else coming?"

I stole a look down what I hoped was a wide enough aisle. "Do you know Travis Nielson?"

"The dude in the chair?" Miles said.

"Yes, I believe he is confined to a wheelchair."

"That guy is a dorkus supreme."

"Miles." Kendra slapped his thigh again.

I hadn't expected Miles's reaction, but it also didn't surprise me. Nothing surprised me anymore on the first day of the Discussions. "Tell me, Miles, why is Travis a dork? Because he has a disability?"

"I don't know, he's just weird. He sometimes rolls by you in the hallway and smells funky. Like that dude from Charlie Brown. Plus he picks his nose—right, Kendra? He's just creepy."

"Be nice, Miles," Kendra said.

"I'm curious. How do you know him? Travis is quite a bit younger than you. He's just a sophomore and you're a senior. And he's new to AHS. This is his first year."

"We have the same lunch and he always seems to end up near me and my guys."

"I'm sure he's nice," Kendra chimed.

Miles mumbled something I couldn't hear and Kendra whispered back in his ear. Then she stood and walked to where I was standing. She picked up a picture book from a nearby table and began leafing through it. "Who else is coming, Mr. Conner? Are you married? How long will we be here?" She finally looked up at me as she asked that last question.

"Yeah, how long?" Miles added. "I've got homework and all."

Kendra looked over her shoulder and whispered something else.

"You'll have time for homework," I said. "Don't worry. We won't be more than an hour. And, Kendra, we will get to all your questions, I promise."

I motioned for her to return to her seat next to Miles and I sat in the white wicker chair near them.

"Who else?" Kendra asked.

"Pardon?"

"Who else is coming?"

"That's it, actually. Just you three."

"That's all?" she said, sounding as if she'd expected two dozen participants.

"Yes, ma'am. Small group this time."

Kendra asked three or four more questions.

Miles pulled his iPhone from his pocket and began texting.

I learned that Kendra was already exhausted just thinking about her senior year.

"Dad says this is my chance to make my mark," she said. "Last chance to be a big fish in a small pond." She pulled out her own cell phone and showed me a grainy photo of her and a member of the Washington Mystics WNBA team. "Speaking of big fish, check out who came to speak to the student council yesterday: Monique Currie. Awesome, huh? Totally amazing lady."

For the next ten minutes, Miles tuned in and out of the chatter only long enough to disagree with Kendra about one point or another. Each time she smiled at him and rolled on, undeterred.

The pair had been dating since freshman year.

Miles had been the star of the JV basketball team as point guard and was quickly promoted to varsity.

Kendra was a cheerleader. "But not like those other girls," she insisted. "I'm not clueless."

"Plus you're way hotter than the others," Miles added without looking up.

"That's not why I'm a cheerleader, Miles."

"Right," he said, looking more in my direction than hers.

I took a deep, long breath. "Kendra, tell me about your parents."

"My mom and dad are divorced. Mom lives in Chantilly with her new boyfriend. But since it's my senior year, we decided it was better for me to stay with Dad and graduate down here."

"Oh. Does she work in Northern Virginia?"

"Not really."

"Does she work?"

"Not really."

"I see. And your father? What does he do?"

"You didn't know? He's the varsity basketball coach."

FIVE

Jade

JADE READS.

My wife reads thick books that require two hands to carry. She also reads novellas, biographies, autobiographies, poetry, fiction, memoirs, and memoirs later proven to be fiction. She reads Condie, Albom, Gilbert, Skye, Sparks, Milne, Cornwell, Koontz, Hosseini, and an occasional Patterson.

She reads books from authors no one but their own mothers have ever heard of.

She reads books recommended by Oprah.

What Jade doesn't do often is watch TV or see movies. Since we met in the late spring of 1997, Jade probably hasn't seen more than five movies in a theater and another dozen at home. So, naturally, our first date was a matinee showing of *Titanic* at a theater in Virginia Beach.

Jade had just graduated from the University of Richmond.

She and three girlfriends celebrated with a long weekend at a beach house rented by Jade's parents.

I celebrated surviving my second year at Virginia Tech with three roommates at a Motel 6 roughly a mile from the same beach.

The four of us first saw the four of them staking out their spots in the mid-morning sun. Honestly, I don't remember much about the other three women—only that they didn't shine like Jade.

I deposited my green canvas bag on the sand, eased the drawstring and pulled out my collapsible chair, and set it up three feet from Jade's. Then, before I sat, I drew a long line with my heel in the sand between our chairs.

Either Jade hadn't noticed or she was an exceptional actress.

"The line is for you," I said, removing my orange Hokies T-shirt and tossing it on the sand by my towel. "Sometimes women get a little, um, overly aggressive when I sit this close without a shirt on." I'd never used this exact approach at the beach, but I had confidence knowing variations on the move had served me well in other venues.

She looked up from her copy of *A People's Tragedy*, made a point of not smiling, studied the line for a moment, and went back to her book.

"Oh, come on," I said. "That's pretty good, you have to admit."

Without making eye contact, she stood up, set her book in her chair, and drew a second line parallel to mine, about six inches apart. Without a word she picked up the book, sat, and resumed reading.

If she'd been trying to turn me off, she'd been wildly unsuccessful. "Let me guess," I said. "The first line is for you, the second line is for me?"

I will never forget the first time I heard her voice.

"Not exactly," she chimed.

Nor the first time she looked right at me and said, "The second one is for your ego."

I clutched my chest. "Ouch! That's a B. That's a solid, *solid* B, maybe even a B-plus if I'm grading on a curve."

The smiles I hoped she'd been suppressing since I first sat all came out at once. "I'm Jade."

I extended my hand, then retracted it. "Whoops, may I?"

She nodded and I leaned across the lines in the sand, tipping my chair sideways on two legs toward her.

We shook.

"My name is Cole Conner. Good to meet you, Jade . . ." I raised my eyebrows and waited for a last name.

It didn't come.

"Jade," I said again. "I like it. Jaaaade. Very classy. Not many women pull off the whole one-name thing."

She folded the corner of her page, shut the book, and set it on top of a red cooler at her side. "First names are free. Last names take work."

"Then consider me on the clock."

This made her shine once again, a smile that had already lit something within me. "What's the book?"

She picked it up again and handed it to me. "It's Figes's *A People's Tragedy*."

"Ah yes," I said, with the authority of a tenured professor and not a college sophomore. "It's a brilliant take on the history of the Russian Revolution."

"You've read it?"

"Just the cover." I pointed to the subtitle and winked.

"It *is* brilliant, in fact." She took the book back. "Just came out and I'm loving it, tragic as it is."

There is a distinct panic that comes when you suddenly realize you might be out of your intellectual league. It can hit in a nightclub, a lecture hall, or a library. Or, apparently, on a beach. "Mind if I ask what kind of girl spends her summer vacation on a beach reading up on the Russian Revolution?"

Her eyes said, *This one.*

Before she could add words to the look, her pals bounced into the moment. "Who's your new friend?" one of them said with her hands on her curvy hips and her index fingers looped playfully around the strings of her purple bikini bottom. The other two straightened their towels and lay on their stomachs.

"This is the honorable Cole Conner," Jade said. She watched my reaction closely.

I rose and politely shook the girl's hand, extraordinarily careful to keep my eyes from drifting south, and returned to my seat and fixed my gaze squarely back where it belonged: on Jade.

Jade noticed. After an awkward moment or two, bikini girl took her place on her towel in line with the others. Before the sand had settled beneath her, my own crew arrived. After the who-are-you and the where-are-you-going-to-college introduc-tions, the three boys had challenged the three girls to volleyball.

They accepted and leapt to their feet.

Jade and I declined.

For an hour, Jade listed the recent books she'd most enjoyed and I countered with the movies that had the best car crashes.

Jade rattled off the countries she'd visited as a child with her parents.

I mentioned the states and Flying J Travel Plazas I'd visited as a child with my own parents.

Jade revealed her freshly awarded degree from the University of Richmond: English with a minor in French.

I was at Tech studying economics with a minor in lazy.

She laughed and said that line would be perfect in the book she hoped to write one day.

"Will I be in your book?"

"That depends on whether I need a villain or not."

I pretended to reach for her. "Muahahahaha." I really don't know what I was thinking.

The awkward look on her face said she didn't either, but she laughed it off anyway. "Don't call us, we'll call you."

At lunchtime, her friends convinced her they needed shade from the comfort of their nearby rented beach house. The boys and I were not invited.

Jade and I finished our conversation as the others gathered their things into giant designer beach bags. We helped them lug their gear toward the boardwalk and I wished Jade hadn't just put on a pair of *Top Gun* aviator-style sunglasses.

"So, Jade, if I asked you out on a real date when you're back in Richmond and I drove over from Blacksburg, what would you say?"

"I'd say why wait."

Five hours later, we met in the lobby of a movie theater not far from the beach.

We saw *Titanic* with DiCaprio and Winslet.

As they crashed into the iceberg, Jade whispered, "You know how this ends, right?"

"The movie or the date?"

"Both."

Later, though she still won't admit it, I'm convinced I saw Jade wipe a tear when Jack drowned in the icy waters.

But mostly, right in the middle of the biggest disaster movie of all time, I saw a future.

SIX

Oakley

MY MOTHER WAS NAMED AFTER THE FAMED SHARPSHOOTER Annie Oakley.

Not because Mother liked guns, but because *her* mother did. And Grandma was quite handy with a rifle. So handy, she shot and killed an intruder with a single bullet in 1953 when Mother was less than a year old.

Grandpa made two guarantees when he left for Korea. He promised Grandma and their newborn daughter they would be safe in his absence. He also promised he would return. Grandpa only kept one. He died navigating a minefield.

Several years later, Grandma remarried and had another daughter. They named her Lisa Ann. She died at age eight.

Grandma's second husband left brokenhearted four months later and, once again, my mom was an only child to a single mother.

Grandma died a few years ago navigating diabetes.

Mom buried her with a small arsenal.

We visit the cemetery frequently. Mother doesn't cry or leave an extra carnation. She just talks.

I just listen.

Mother met my father and despite a long, occasionally rocky courtship, they were married in 1975.

Dad worked as an accountant until a client, Joe Thomas, convinced him to try his hand at radio. Dad began appearing as a guest on Joe's show at WCHV until getting his very own slot. Almost overnight, Dad went from accountant to radio guest to radio host.

He readily admitted that he'd never been so excited to get up in the morning.

It was no secret that Dad loved the radio business because it gave him a forum to discuss his daily Seventeen Second Miracles. He even launched a short, regular segment where he took anonymous calls from listeners who wanted to report their daily miracles.

Mother loved and supported him at every unpredictable turn.

And he supported her.

When the radio business wasn't lucrative enough to support us, Mother got a job in the human resources office at the university. Dad could tell she wasn't content, and one Monday morning hid her car keys while she ate breakfast.

"You're not happy, sweetheart."

"Of course I am," she contested.

"No, you're not. You deserve to love your job as much as I do, and it's my fault our standard of living changed." He took her hand. "You're miserable in that cubicle."

"It's a job, Rex. And it keeps juice on the table." She took another sip of hers and stood to begin clearing the dishes.

"I can't go to the radio station every day and know you're slogging along across town to earn a paycheck, just because I turned in my accounting brain for this one. It's not fair to you."

By then, Mother was digging through her purse and coat pockets.

"Honey, have you seen my keys?"

They fussed at each other for a few minutes, mostly in jest, as I readied for school. Eventually Mother agreed to look for another job in exchange for her keys and a kiss.

Dad complied, and he held her to the deal.

The result was a career for my mother in real estate. We all learned that being an agent was a lifestyle and skill set that suited Mother well. She loves people and loves being in motion. It's a career she continues to thrive in today.

We both remember the first time we were riding in the car and heard Dad promote her on the air.

"OK, Charlottesville, you've heard me advertise a lot of companies and good causes on this show. But this one means more to me than any other and she's a brand-new advertiser. I want to introduce you to one of the newest and finest real estate agents serving our city. She's with Stephen Fountain Realty, and she's tall, talented, and, if I do say so myself, mighty easy on the eyes. She's my wife, Oakley Conner, and she's got a wonderful three-bedroom home in Crozet she's dying to show you. Go see her at the agency's offices on Ivy Road or call 540-325-8219. Now, before you call the station, let me just tell you we don't do freebies at WCHV. This commercial was paid for at the same rate any advertiser would pay. The only difference is I got to kiss the client good-bye this morning."

I turned down the volume and looked over at Mother. She stared straight ahead with tears in her eyes and a smile on her face. "Are you OK?"

"Yes, Cole."

"Are you happy?"

"Very."

"With Dad's commercial?"

"No, dear, with Dad."

I wasn't sure what she meant, but I wouldn't have to admit that. Mom was the good kind of mother who could just tell.

"I've always been happy, Cole, because you and your father are at my side."

"But are you happier now? Happy to leave the house for work every day? Like Dad said?"

"Will you two still be there every day when I get home?"

"Well, yeah, sure we will."

"Then I couldn't be happier."

SEVEN

Travis

THEY PULLED UP FIFTEEN MINUTES LATE.

We could see out a side window into the alley next to the store. We all stood up to get a better look.

The white van that settled into the handicapped parking spot had red-and-orange flames that started just above the grill, sprayed across the hood, and wrapped around the left and right, ending just below the front-door handles.

"That's him," Miles said, still texting.

"You're sure?" I asked.

"One hundred."

I hesitated. "Excuse me?"

"Percent," Kendra added for him.

"Ah. Good then. I know you both will be kind."

Together we watched his mother get out, walk around the van, wave pleasantly to us through the window, and open the side door. A silver hydraulic lift churned to life and a ramp delivered Travis's wheelchair to the sidewalk.

From where we stood, it sounded as if Travis's mother asked if he wanted her to walk him into the store. While we couldn't be completely certain of the question, the answer was indisputable: an emphatic *no*.

Miles whispered something in Kendra's ear, and I moved to the front door to greet Travis Nielson for the first time.

"Do you need me?" his mother called to him as the platform vanished back into the belly of the van and she shut the side door.

Travis didn't answer.

"Trav?" she called again, fidgeting with her car keys.

By then Travis had turned the corner and was nearly to the store entrance. He wore a Washington Redskins ball cap cocked a few degrees right of center, a Clinton Portis jersey, grey sweatpants, and a thick gold chain around his neck.

His mother, now standing where we could see her, called out, "Good-bye, Trav."

When he didn't answer, she waved to me and disappeared back into the alley.

"Wait," I said and jogged past Travis toward her. "I wanted to meet you. I'm Cole Conner."

When I offered my hand, she pretended she didn't see it and hugged me instead. "It's so nice to meet you, Mr. Conner. Thank you for inviting Travis to be here."

"You're welcome, Mrs. Nielson. But you should thank

Mr. Buhl from the high school. He's the one who made the recommendation."

"Fine then, Mr. Conner." Her voice cracked. "I am grateful to you both."

I said good-bye, invited her to return at six-thirty to pick up her son, and returned to help Travis navigate his way back to the Reading Corner.

Travis was already parked across from Miles and Kendra, his back right up against Rudolph. He was, I noticed, as far away from them as he could get without rolling into the little bathroom.

"How was the aisle?" I said as I arrived at the group.

"Too narrow," Travis answered without looking at me.

"I'm sorry. You made it through OK, though?"

"Do you see me sitting here?"

Miles looked at me and mouthed, *Told you.*

I ignored the moment and offered my hand to Travis. "My name is Mr. Conner. It's a pleasure to meet you."

Instead of taking my hand, he balled up his fist and said, "Pound it, man."

"No thank you, Travis. I'd prefer to *shake* your hand." I kept my hand out.

Travis looked at Miles, who rolled his eyes.

Then he looked to Kendra, who had her hands folded delicately in her lap and her eyes draped with pity.

Finally Travis shook my hand, gripping it as firmly as he probably could but looking at my chest and not my eyes.

I looked down at him and held his hand equally tightly until he made eye contact. "Thank you, Travis," I said when he finally looked up.

"Whatever," he whispered.

"Do you know everyone, Travis?"

"I've seen them around," he said.

"Why don't we do introductions anyway, all right? You all know me now. I'm Mr. Conner, and this my wife's store." I stretched my arms out in a proud gesture of semi-ownership and then nodded at Miles.

"Miles," he said.

"And my name is Kendra Wilson."

"Who?" Travis asked.

"Why don't you come a little closer and find out," I answered. He pushed forward on his wheels and cut the distance in half.

"That's better. This is Kendra Wilson."

Travis flashed some hand sign at her. "Waddup."

"And now you. Would you like to introduce yourself?"

"Name is Trav. Or T. Whatever is fine with me."

"Thank you, Travis." As I took my seat, I considered commenting on Travis's fifteen-minutes-late arrival and how I hoped to start on time each week. But given the already awkward air in the Reading Corner, I chose to simply glance at my watch and hold the look until I thought he'd seen.

"So," I began, "let's see those pocket watches."

EIGHT

Seventeen Seconds

LIKE EVERY YEAR, THE FIRST SESSION STARTS WITH STARING.

The intros were complete, the room was still, and three teens sat before me, completely unaware of why they were there. Unfortunately, I couldn't tell them; I didn't have a clue either.

They held their pocket watches and looked at me with young eyes and a thousand questions. After so many years and so many students, even on the first day I could go around the room and already tell them what they were thinking. There is a blend of confusion and anxiety on their faces.

I suppose it's been on my face, too.

I cleared my throat. "I'm so glad you're all here." No matter how many times I run the Discussions, I'm always as nervous as they are. "I know you have many questions—"

Kendra's hand shot up.

I waved her off. "Hang tight."

Miles snickered at her and her cheeks flushed.

"Let's start with the pocket watch." The kids were already holding them; everyone except for Miles. He appeared to be playing a game on his iPhone and Kendra was holding both their watches. I'd let Travis's tardiness go, but I feared Miles would never engage in the Discussions if I didn't set an early standard. "Miles, would you mind putting the phone away?"

His expression suggested either he wasn't used to such bold direction, or I didn't know him nearly well enough to make such a request. It was probably some of both. He fiddled an extra second and, without answering, slid the phone back into his jeans' pocket.

"Thank you. I appreciate it, Miles." I sat a little straighter and inched up to the edge of my chair. "I'd like to know what all of you thought when you opened your invitation envelope and found a watch." I looked at each of them. It's always been helpful to have someone willing to go first, especially on Day One, and it was obvious Kendra was it. "Kendra?"

"I was really curious. Right, Miles? I called him immediately. I was in the kitchen because that's where my mom stacks the mail every day. By the intercom base. Miles was in his car still driving home. Then when he got home, he called me back and said he had gotten one, too."

"All right," I steered, "but what did you *think*? Besides being curious?"

She looked at the watch. "I noticed how pretty it is. So detailed. I like the designs on it. Actually, I admit that I thought it was from Miles at first, before I read the note."

"That's fair. Thank you."

"How about you, Travis?"

Travis was spinning the watch on its chain. "I thought . . . Whatever. Cool watch."

"Anything else?"

He shrugged.

Miles was sitting low in the love seat, his neck resting against a pillow he had borrowed from another chair. His long legs were crossed with one ankle resting on the other thigh. They formed a triangle almost big enough to dunk a basketball through.

"Miles, what about you?"

He sat up and took the watch from Kendra. "I thought it looked like my grandpa's watch."

"Really?" I asked.

"He had one he used to carry a lot."

"That's neat, Miles. Does he still have it?"

"He's dead."

"I'm sorry."

"It's all good," he said, and Kendra took his hand, interlocking her fingers with his.

I looked back at Travis. "Did any of you consider not coming?"

"Duh," Travis said.

"Really?"

"I was like, this ain't a requirement. Plus it's three days a week."

"But you came," I said, and I instantly regretted it because I knew he wouldn't be able to resist.

He hesitated, but only long enough for Miles and Kendra to look at him. "Do you see me sitting here?"

I sighed. "I do. And I'm glad." I retrieved a watch from my own pocket and held it up. "I got one, too."

"In the mail?" Kendra asked.

"No, I got this from my father when I was about your age. It's one of my most prized possessions."

"Why?" Kendra asked.

"Well, first, because my dad gave it to me. And I know it meant a lot to him. It *reminds* me of him."

"Is he dead?" Travis asked.

"We'll get to that." I could sense another question on his lips, but he swallowed it.

"Do we get to keep these?" The question came from Kendra. That specific question always comes early.

"If you earn it, yes."

"How?" At some point Kendra had pulled a small, matching Vera Bradley pen and notebook from her Vera Bradley purse.

"We'll get to that, too." I winked.

Kendra started to write, then looked up at me and grinned an apology.

"I'd like you all to open the watch and look at the face," I instructed. "They should already be set to the correct time."

Kendra checked the time against her yellow Swatch.

The boys flipped open their cell phones to do the same.

"Now I want you to do something for me. I want you to watch the second hand. Watch it circle the face. When I say 'start,' I want you to follow the second hand and—in your heads—count out seventeen seconds."

All three students were studying their watches. I let the quiet build longer than usual. After forty-five seconds, I said quietly, "Start."

1—2—3—4—5—6—7—8—9—10—11—12—13—14—15—16—17.

When they finished, they all looked at me with the same question: *And?*

"That's not much time, is it?" I said.

"I thought it felt like forever," said Kendra.

"Miles, what did seventeen seconds feel like to you?"

"Uh"—he looked down at the watch face again—"like not much time, actually."

I made eye contact with each. "Travis, Miles, Kendra, I know you're all very curious about why I invited you here. What is this all about? If I were you, I'd be brimming with questions. Why me? Why did Principal Buhl pick me?"

"So?" Travis interrupted my rhythm.

"I don't know, Travis. I don't know why *any* of you were selected. That's the magic of our time together. We'll discover that as a group over the course of our Discussions. What I *do* know is what I want you to remember about our first meeting."

I held my watch up and swung it very gently on its chain. "Seventeen seconds. That's all it takes to change a life. And together during these Discussions, we're going to find out how."

"Mr. Conner," Kendra said. "Your invitation from the mail said these were about the Seventeen Second Miracle. So what's the miracle?"

"Come on Wednesday. Same time."

"And if we don't?" Miles asked.

"Then it will be our loss."

I stood up, again looked them each in the eye, and thanked them for coming. Then I invited them to chat among themselves until Travis's mother arrived. When she did, they would all be dismissed.

I said good-bye and went to see if Jade was in the back. As I shut the "employees only" door behind me, I said to myself, "If they all come back, *that* will be the miracle."

NINE

The Wait

IF DELIVERY DAY IS AMONG MY FAVORITES OF THE YEAR, THE days between the first and second Discussion are among the worst.

After the students left, I sat in Jade's tiny office and gave her the rundown on each student. And though it was still very early, we speculated on why Principal Buhl might have specifically recommended them for the program.

I could ask him, of course, but I knew he wouldn't tell me. He'd simply say what he'd said in years past: "You and the kids will figure it out, Cole, just the way your father would have liked it. And, if I'm candid, I'm not always sure I know either."

I'd offer a faux protest and he'd slip into a story about my father and their exploits together. And before long, I could leave the room and he wouldn't even notice.

After dinner out, Jade spent a couple more hours in the bookstore. She offered to go home with me, knowing from past years how anxious I would be. But I knew her Christmas season was about to kick off, and, honestly, I didn't feel good about keeping her from the only thing in life she loved with the same passion as she loved me.

Paper Gem Books is her baby. Perhaps, in part, because we couldn't have any of our own.

I think Jade threw herself into books sometime around her third birthday and never quit.

Until the Discussions, I'd never thrown myself into anything but pools and sleeping in.

Like my father, I'd taken what felt like the obligatory march into accounting with a natural knack for numbers. I didn't do it because I had a longing for sixteen-hour days and federal tax code; I did it because it came easy to me. After my college graduation and our wedding, both happening the same spring, I spent two tax seasons with a second-tier firm in Northern Virginia while Jade worked at Politics & Prose Bookstore in D.C. But traffic and tax forms conspired against me. I will die grateful that Jade didn't fight me when I suggested a move to the more serene lifestyle of Charlottesville.

We spent our first year in Charlottesville in an apartment off Barrack's Road. Neither of us would deny that we'd enjoyed the one-bedroom apartment with its shag carpet and peeling green-and-orange linoleum. But we also couldn't deny that on the day when her parents offered the cash for a down payment on our first home, we politely offered to consider it, then raced to see eight homes before the sun set.

We'd narrowed it to two homes, both on Jefferson Park Avenue, a major artery rich with history and character.

One of the homes was recently remodeled with new plumbing, flooring, and windows.

The other needed all three.

One had a roof so recently replaced that the sun still sparkled off the sand in the brand-new shingles.

The other had an older roof that Jade conjectured was constructed by the same patriots who built the Rotunda on campus at the University of Virginia in 1826.

One had a price tag we could not afford.

The other became ours.

We moved in and chose our battles. Not with one another, but with the home. New paint, cabinets, windows, closet doors, and other odds and ends found their turn. But the last improvement was my favorite.

I'd driven around town for two days taking pictures of other people's porches before I presented the options to Jade over burritos at Guadalajara's.

"All that for a porch? I'm surprised you didn't get shot," Jade said. "Or worse, arrested."

"Fear not." I breathed on and rubbed my knuckles against my chest. "I was discreet."

"Uh-huh." Jade ripped off a piece of tortilla and dipped it in the hot salsa we shared in the middle of the table.

"So here's what I like best." I arranged two photos between us and set another twenty off to the side. "We'll call these two the porch showcase showdown."

"Oh boy. Here we go." Jade wiped her mouth and slid her plate away.

I tapped the photo on her left. "This is my favorite, by far. It's the best fit for our house and architecture; it's huge; it will look great and, most important, you will look great on it."

Jade kept her head down but looked up at me and smiled. "That's the best you've got? I'll look great on it?"

"Not bad, right?"

She smiled. "Yeah, not bad."

I put my hand on the losing porch photo and began to move it toward the other stack of losers when she pressed her thumb down on the corner and forced it back to its place next to the other. "Not so fast, Bob Barker. What did you like about this one?"

"Huh?" Actually, I hadn't really liked much about it.

"This one," she pressed. "What made this one also a showcase showdown porch?"

I spun the picture around on the tabletop and examined it. "Well. I like that it's not screened in. It's wide-open. Friendly. I know that means we'll get some summertime bugs, but the screened porches just aren't as inviting."

"What else?"

"And the columns are stone. I like that, too. That might be the best feature."

She tapped the first photo again. "And this one. What specifically do we like about it?"

"I love the brick. Don't you? See how aged it is? It's a good look on a home like ours. Very authentic Charlottesville. Very downtown. And look at the support columns. They're stone, too, but they're composite. Look at how each smaller stone builds on the other, very uneven, imperfect, but still strong. Must be a thousand rocks in each one."

"And?"

"And it's also open, no screens, plus it's one of the biggest wraparounds I've seen, which you know I love, and you can't see here but it has the classic Southern blue-painted ceiling."

Jade turned the picture back around and took her turn studying it. "Can we afford it?" she asked.

"Are there still checks in the checkbook?"

She flicked a tortilla chip at me.

"It's not going to be cheap, no, but I think we can make it work. And it's going to add value to the place, definitely."

Her eyes were still fixed on the photo, but I could tell she wasn't actually looking at it anymore.

I took a drink of my second sangria. "It speaks to me, Jade. I see you and I hiding in chairs in the corner watching the sunset. Your hair is teasing your shoulders and your bare legs are draped over mine. And maybe, just maybe, you're holding our baby."

Jade put her elbows on the table and rested her chin on her clenched fists. Then she stared into my eyes with a look that said: *I couldn't care less what the porch looks like, as long as we're on it together.*

"Well?" I asked.

"All right, Bob, we have a winner. This one." She picked up the photo and held it with both hands high overhead like a proud lion cub. "This, this is the one." She spoke even louder, her voice a blend of John Madden and Martin Luther King. "This is the porch we shall build! It is the circle of life!"

As she began to hum, I leaned across the table to kiss her.

"Oh my, Mr. Barker, please!"

But I didn't answer. My mind was already preparing the front of the house for construction of our porch. It started out as our porch but spent a long, sad time as *my* porch.

While I oversaw construction, Jade took a job at a used bookstore near campus.

I continued doing taxes, this time under my own shingle, and branched into payroll, benefits, and eventually became licensed and certified to handle some investment and estate planning. I found that clients trusted me, sometimes surprisingly fast.

I didn't love the work, still don't, but I loved the people. Still do.

Jade says clients gravitate to me because I treat them well and because I serve them constantly. She believes that's my reputation.

I think she's half-right. I do think a reputation brings them to me. But it's not *my* reputation; it's Dad's. Though he's been gone from the coffee shops and Jade's bookstore for several years, he's still a much-loved and oft-discussed figure around town. The radio station still displays his cheesy autographed headshot in the lobby.

I'm not the only one anxious on the days between Discussions, particularly the first few each year. The days themselves seem distracted, passing for me at different speeds, the sun seeming to linger in the sky too long most days. Then suddenly one day it's dark before I've had a chance to appreciate its place in the skyline.

I spend time between Discussions performing my own daily Seventeen Second Miracles. It's a slower time of year for most of my clients, and I'm able to spend less time at the office than during other months. Still, to keep the days folding one to the next, like playing cards in a deck too fat to shuffle at once, I drop by the office every day for small visits to say hello and put out fires.

The more visits I pay, the faster the days pass through my hands.

The faster the days pass through my hands, the faster I get back to the store for my next Discussion.

My office is downtown on High Street. Once, maybe twice a week, I walk to Paper Gems and eat lunch with Jade. I watch as she helps a customer or explains the magic of a rare book to one of her two part-time employees. There are few things I'd rather do than sit in the wicker chair in the back corner and watch her play with her books.

She moves with grace around the store, like a concert pianist playing on her feet. Her shelves of books are like keys on a piano only she knows how to play. She gushes over the classics from Tolkien, Morrison, Fitzgerald, Nabokov, and Orwell. She nearly gets emotional selling Booker T. Washington's *Up from Slavery*.

The customer hugs her.

As I watch I'm reminded, with no small measure of pain, that for too long I took that dance for granted. I finally understand that this dance, this recital, this flawless performance, isn't a performance at all. It is real. She has books.

I have the miracles.

In time, another satisfied customer thanks her, pays for their book, thanks her again, and disappears out the door and into the crowd, those unfortunate souls who didn't have tickets for her latest performance.

TEN

History

ALL THREE ARRIVED AT ONCE.

I watched from a black metal bench across from the store.

At 5:35 P.M., Miles and Kendra pulled up in his black Saab and were able to find a parking space less than a block away.

Miles hopped out and walked toward Paper Gems.

Travis showed up again in his mother's van. His mother opened the side door, lowered his chair, said good-bye, and watched him roll away.

Only when the van pulled out did I realize that Kendra had stopped to talk to a woman window-shopping along the pedestrian mall that began with Paper Gems. She was walking her twin bichon frise puppies. Kendra got on one knee and petted them both.

Miles had noticed, too, and yelled from the front door. "K, we're starting soon. Come on."

"It's OK, Miles," I offered as I walked across the street that hadn't seen a car in more than thirty years. "Let her say hello." He shoved his hands in his pockets and leaned against the rough stone entryway.

We followed Kendra into the store, where Miles took a seat in the love seat again and Travis parked himself in the same place as Monday. Rudolph peered around him as if trying to join our group. Kendra settled in so close to Miles that the love seat looked like it could seat a couple more teenagers.

"You know what's interesting," I said. "Every year, my students gravitate to the same places each session. In this big corner of the store with plenty of stools, chairs, that love seat, and even Santa's big red chair to choose from, we always end up in the same places. Did anyone notice that?"

"I did," Kendra said. "I think it's comfortable that way."

"Why?" I asked.

"It just is," she continued. "We do it at school, too. Hardly ever do we have assigned seats, but we just go back to the same places all the time. Even at lunch."

"Travis." I turned to him. "Have you ever noticed this?"

"I guess."

"What went through your mind when you came to a stop at the same place as last time?"

"Who knows. It just happened that way. I guess I like seeing the street."

"That's *very* interesting." I meant it. He sat in the only place where he could see out the window into the alley and through the store out the front doors.

"Before we start, let's talk about last time. Let's have everyone name one thing we talked about. Travis?"

"You showed your pop's watch."

"Excellent. How about you, Mil—"

"—and you told us," Travis interrupted, "that we could maybe keep it."

"That's correct. I did. I said you'd have a chance to *earn* it. Well said."

Kendra jumped in. "You also had us count out seventeen seconds, to see how long it was, right?"

"That's correct. Miles?"

He pulled his pocket watch out of his pocket and held it up. "You said seventeen seconds could change a life."

"Outstanding. I said exactly that, didn't I?"

Miles slipped the watch back into his pocket.

I stood up, walked across the room, and sat on a padded bar stool.

Travis turned his left wheel slightly to watch me.

"Here's what *I* remember. You guys were great. You showed up here without any explanation. Just a note and a watch. And you came back, which was the first big test."

Miles pumped his fist and Kendra smiled.

"So you deserve some answers, don't you?"

"Straight up," Travis said, and I noticed he was wearing a different gold chain than Monday.

"Straight up?" I repeated.

He pounded his chest and gave me a peace sign.

"OK then, here it is, straight up." I made a lame attempt to pound my chest back at him. "I'm in finance, I own a small firm, and my wife owns and runs this bookstore."

Blank stares.

"Mrs. Conner and I have lived in Charlottesville for over ten years. I went to college at Virginia Tech in Blacksburg and she went to the University of Richmond. We met at the beach, fell in love, got married, lived in Northern Virginia for a bit, and then settled down here. We love this area."

Miles made a subtle reach for his phone, but a look from Kendra ended the maneuver.

"Charlottesville is the kind of town that if you embrace her, well, she accepts you and treats you as a native, as if you were born right down the road at Martha Jefferson Hospital—even if you weren't. It's the spirit of Jefferson, I think. It's an engaging city, an entrepreneurial city, a city of learning and service."

"Dude, you sound like a commercial," Travis said and the others laughed.

I threw my hands in the air. "What can I say? This is my kind of town." I moved back to my chair and motioned for Travis to approach.

He rolled a few feet closer.

"I told you three last time that I don't know why you're here, right?"

Three heads bobbed up and down.

"But what I do know is why *I* am here." With my right index finger, I made a circle over my head. "This corner. This corner of Paper Gems was built for a very specific purpose. Any ideas?"

"Wheelchair obstacle course," Travis said.

"That's just a side benefit." I gave him a sly smile. "This is a place for stories. Fictional stories, true stories, kids' stories, short stories. Stories about Seventeen Second Miracles." My voice trailed off at the end as highlights of Discussions past ran through my mind.

The year I had Joe Wobbe. He was a D or worse student on the verge of dropping out of AHS for trade school until the Discussions began to change his heart. I can still smell the smoked salmon he made for Jade and me as a thank-you. I've heard he owns his own steakhouse now in Woodstock. *One of these days,* I promised myself, *we'll surprise him.*

A year later, maybe two, Jade became close to a young lady we'd learned was invited to the Discussions as a way, in part, to get away from a boyfriend with a toxic temper. She finally left the young man, but only after he left her with a bloodied lip and a swollen eye. She and Jade still talk once every couple months. She teaches journalism at Monticello High School.

"Uh, Mr. Conner, are you OK?" Kendra's eyes were concerned.

I must have drifted a moment too long. "Never better. I just love this place."

"Dude." Travis stepped in. "You might want to lay off the story love. It's creepy."

"True that," Miles added.

I was back on my feet again. "I don't know quite how to explain it, there's just something special about it. Would you like to know how many students have been invited to attend these Discussions?" There's never a point waiting for an answer to that one. "Let's see, five years here, five years on the porch before that, five or six students on average every session—that's at least fifty."

Kendra said, "Mr. Conner, you said you knew why *you* were here. But you didn't really tell *us*."

"It's rather simple. I'm here because I have a story to tell. More like stories, really."

"Stories about what?" Kendra persisted.

"Stories about a miraculous life. A miraculous journey. Stories that changed my life forever."

"So." Travis said what the other two were probably thinking.

"So they just might change your lives, too."

Miles removed his arm from Kendra's shoulder and leaned forward. "Who says our lives need changing anyway?"

"That's a fair question. I told you already that I don't know why you were chosen. I only know that Principal Buhl must think extremely highly of each of you for you to be here."

"What do we get out of it?" Travis wheeled even closer and I turned to face him.

"Out of what?"

"Out of coming three times a week. What else?"

"You get an education. And a letter from me to whatever college you decide to attend."

Kendra ignored the latter point. "An education of what? Of the Seventeen Second Miracle?" Kendra asked.

"That's right."

"And what is it?"

"The miracle?"
She nodded.
"Are you sure you're ready?" I asked.
Kendra: "Yes."
Travis: "Duh."
Miles: "Uh-huh."
"Then let's get started."

ELEVEN

Lifeguards

IT'S AS IF I'D BEEN LAKESIDE THAT LATE-SUMMER DAY.

"As I've already said, we're not here today because of *me*. This journey, this time together, it's not about Cole Conner. It's about my father, Rex Conner, and the lessons he learned and taught. It's about his legacy and how best to pass it on. And listen, it's perfectly all right if you don't appreciate our Discussions right away. I sure didn't appreciate the lessons when I first heard and saw them for myself. In fact, I had been married for several years before I really got it. But promise me that no matter what, you will all come back on Friday."

They stared at me.

"Promise?"

"Well, *I* do," Kendra said with conviction.

Miles and Travis actually made eye contact. Then they both looked at me and nodded.

I began the story that had brought us together in the first place:

"My father was a lifeguard when he was your age. He loved the water, the freedom of it all. Any of you ever been to Chris Greene Lake out by the airport? That was his turf. The lake hadn't even been open a full year when he got the job."

I stood up and moved back to the stool. I turned around and looked at Miles and Kendra.

"Dad met his first girlfriend that summer. He called her Sparks."

Miles's eyes widened. "Her name was Sparks?"

"No, I said he *called* her Sparks. He said that the first time he saw her, late one hot summer afternoon, he saw sparks all around her, like an aura. That's how beautiful she was."

Kendra sighed. Loudly. "That's the sweetest thing I've ever heard in my whole entire life."

"What? You want a nickname?" Miles asked without looking at her. His eyes were darting back and forth between Travis and me.

Kendra kept her eyes on me and simply shook her head. "Sorry for interrupting, Mr. Conner."

Miles slumped back down into the cushions and gazed up at the ceiling.

"Sparks and my father fell into love. Or some version of it anyway. They were, after all, *very* young. My father worked as many shifts at the lake as he could get. Partly for the money, but mostly so he had an excuse to see her. I remember him telling me he almost felt guilty for the job, because he got paid to admire her in a swimsuit."

"Nice call," Travis said, and Kendra rolled her eyes, not for the first or last time that day.

"Sparks had a younger sister. Dad called her Flick. Perhaps you can imagine why. She looked like her sister, just younger and innocent. One day, no doubt, she would be as stunning and bright-eyed as her attractive, older sister. But back then, that summer, she was still just a flick."

"A flick of a flame," Kendra offered. "Not a full spark yet."

"Exactly." I pointed at her for emphasis.

She sighed again, but not as loud and with less effect than the first time.

I took a deep breath, too, and told the story.

When I described the party and the gifts and the cake, Kendra's eyes lit up like a little girl's.

"I love birthday parties," she said.

When I explained Dad's complete devotion to Sparks, and his infatuation with her magazine-model good looks, Miles said, "Your old man was a stud. Sweet."

Later, when I described Flick's struggle in the deeper water and my father's frantic efforts to tow her lifeless blue body to shore, Travis pulled his hat down enough to shield his eyes.

"Imagine now, if you can, being in my father's place on the shore of the lake that day. Can you? Can you picture Flick's mother standing in front of you? Pounding her fist on your chest? She screamed at him, 'Rex Conner, you just couldn't keep your hands to yourself, could you?'"

Kendra and I had tears on our cheeks. "But she lived, right, Mr. Conner?" Her hands went to her face.

Miles sat stiff.

Travis was gripping the wheels of his chair and staring down at his lap.

"That's the Seventeen Second Miracle, right?" Kendra pled. "That Flick lived. That she came back."

"No," I whispered. "Flick was dead."

TWELVE

Silence

THE SILENCE SETTLED.

Every time I've told my father's story, there has been a silence that settles across the group, like morning fog that everyone knows will burn off eventually, but that cannot be rushed.

Only time lifts it.

As I'd done in the past, I finished the story and excused myself. Moments later, I returned with four cold sodas and a box of Kleenex.

Without speaking, Kendra took two Kleenex and a Diet Coke.

Miles and Travis took Dr Peppers.

I took the remaining Diet Coke and sat.

The silence settled.

Miles began to rub Kendra's back as she dabbed at her eyes with a tissue.

Travis opened his can of Dr Pepper, took a long drink, and secured the can between his knees. Then he wheeled himself backward, spun, and rolled across to the opposite corner of the reading area.

I wondered where his mind was.

I wondered, too, what Miles and Kendra were thinking as their eyes avoided mine.

Kendra wiped her eyes and nose and gazed out the window at the alley.

Miles began fidgeting with his phone. Not using it, just flipping it around nervously in his fingers.

I glanced at my watch and realized Travis's mother would soon return for him.

Kendra opened her Diet Coke, took a dainty sip, and put her head on Miles's shoulder. She inhaled and slowly her eyes closed.

"You all right, Kendra?"

She nodded.

I took a sip of my drink.

"Travis, what are you feeling right now?"

He shrugged and ran his finger along the top of his soda can.

Miles's phone rang. He glanced at the screen, then to me, and rested it back on his knee.

"How about you, Miles? You want to share something?"

He acted as if he hadn't heard me, and the silence settled.

I heard reverent tapping on the window and looked to my left.

Jade waved, blew me a kiss, and put her thumb-and-pinkie phone to her head.

After a minute or two, I saw her green Vespa buzz past the window and down the alley.

I walked to the window and watched her until she turned the corner, bound for home and a kitchen full of things she would turn into a wonderful dinner for two.

I set my drink on a square table near my chair and leaned back, stretching my arms high and locking my fingers behind my head.

My eyes closed.

Once again, in my manufactured darkness, I saw my father telling me about a lake, a pretty girl, and a drowning.

In my mind's rerun version, my mother was there beside him the first time he told me of his legacy. She cried at his side on our plaid couch, and she seemed to me not just an audience member, but a participant in my father's grief.

A few details remain brilliantly clear, like well-preserved color photos pasted on the memory's aging, watercolor collage: the wood paneling that surrounded us in our family's living room; the leather journal Dad clutched; his loosened tie knot.

Even more memorable were the tears she did not wipe. As Dad described Flick's last moments and the furious efforts to save her, Mother's tears stuck to her cheeks like little diamonds. I remember wondering why she didn't dab them away.

I spent a few minutes trying to convince myself of that night's place in history. With my eyes still closed tight, I thought: *Yes, that was, in fact, the very first time my mother and father sat me down to tell me the story that changed countless lives.*

But, like every time before, the story was such a part of my life, my blood, my childhood, I could not and cannot be certain that was its debut. Mother has never been confident one way or another, and I've given up wishing I could ask my father himself.

I opened my eyes and sat up.

Miles and Kendra were whispering to one another.

I noticed that Travis had started down the aisle and parked near the store entrance. His back was to us, his eyes locked on the corner where his mother would appear from the alley.

I stood and moved toward the entrance. As I decided whether to walk out and say good-bye, Travis pushed his way out the door. I followed him to the corner and tossed my right hand in the air at his mother.

She waved back. As quickly as she'd arrived, she was gone, turning onto Main Street and away from me.

Kendra and Miles climbed out of the love seat and each shook my hand when I offered it. Then with a quiet good-bye, they made their way down the street; into Miles's Saab; and back to the blissful adolescence of friends, basketball, and cheerleading.

And, I hoped, to safe dry land.

THIRTEEN

Grey

GREY.

That was how my father described the days after Flick's death.
Everything was grey.

The suits, the casket, the rain that fell the afternoon they laid
her to rest in a church cemetery in the southern part of Albemarle County.

Grey dresses.

Grey umbrellas.

Grey tears on his pillow every night for months.

Grey chairs in the waiting room of the therapist's office.

Grey morning air. Grey chalkboards. Grey textbooks.

Grey-framed reading glasses on Flick's mother the afternoon
my father showed up at her front door to apologize face-to-face.
He'd written a few unanswered letters, sobbed out *I'm sorry* on
her shoulder more than once during the week of the funeral,

and sent flowers with a tiny apology written on an even tinier condolence card.

She'd neither accepted his apologies nor dismissed them. She'd simply not engaged with him long enough to do either.

Sparks and my father remained friends, but both sensed their summer teen romance had been buried with Flick. They walked the school halls in a daze. They rode to the lake together and sat on the sand near the spot Flick stepped from one reality to another.

They cried.

They laughed.

They blamed themselves.

They grieved together.

Most of Dad's high school friends didn't know how to talk to him or be around him. So they did neither.

Sparks's friends were warmer and supportive. Most of them blamed my father for Sparks's and her family's suffering. It helped that many had also known and loved Flick.

So in the early weeks of the school year, they wept with her in the girls' bathroom between classes. They surrounded her at lunch, invited her to dances, concerts, and movies. And they also encouraged her to make a clean break from my father.

It saved his life—literally—that she didn't.

Dad dropped out of sports, quit the yearbook staff, and did just enough homework to keep his guidance counselor at school satisfied and his parents from lecturing him. Everyone knew his struggles and everyone sympathized.

To his face, they offered a smile and occasional hug. But when he passed by them in the office or hallways they whispered in authoritative tones:

He wasn't paying any attention.

He watched her die.

He must feel so guilty.

So very, very guilty.

She was only eight.

I heard he hasn't even spoken to her mother.

I think the sister is doing even better than Rex.

I couldn't live with myself.

Dad grew accustomed to the sound track around him, mostly from adults who thought they knew better. After a particularly energetic fight with Sparks, one that ended in profanity and a slap across Dad's face, he drove to Chris Greene Lake with a stolen bottle of whiskey and a small bottle of a generic cleaner he assumed was deadly.

He drank both.

Hours later, with dawn's mist hovering across the lake's glassy surface, Sparks found him unconscious in a pool of grey vomit atop a picnic table.

She drove him to the hospital, waited for him to recover, and slapped him again.

FOURTEEN

Absence

5:30.

5:45.

6:05.

"He's not coming, Mr. Conner." Kendra's voice was kind, mature.

I stood a final time and looked down the alley; still no sign of Travis's flame-adorned van. "I'm afraid you're right," I conceded. "And I owe you both an apology for waiting so long. We should have started a half hour ago."

"It's OK. Right, Miles?"

"Sure." Miles was in the same position he'd been in the first two sessions. Only his wardrobe had changed. He wore a grey hoodie, nice jeans, and running shoes without socks.

Kendra wore khakis and an AHS sweatshirt.

She and Miles sat on the love seat and I faced them from my

padded wicker chair, still at an angle to allow room for Travis's wheelchair to join the circle. Just in case.

"Well, you two, normally this week I'd want to talk more about my dad's experiences at the lake that day and get your reactions, discuss what it all means today. But without Travis here, maybe we can hold off on that until next time?"

Miles shrugged.

"Whatever you think is best," Kendra offered. "I do have lots of questions, though."

"I bet you do." I smiled for the first time since realizing Travis probably wasn't coming, and I knew somewhere in her purse she was probably hauling around a notebook with a bulleted list of inquiries.

A loud delivery truck lumbered down the alley and I stole a look. "Actually I have some questions, too. And after all, these are called *Discussions*, right?"

Kendra sat a little straighter.

"Miles," I began, "here's one for you. Can you tell me what you like about Kendra?"

They *both* sat a little straighter.

"What do you mean?"

"I mean, what do you like about her? What attracts you to her?"

He flung his arm around her. "Everything. She's awesome."

Kendra patted his thigh.

"Yes, she *is* awesome, isn't she? But give me specifics. What, precisely, do you most appreciate about her?"

Miles shifted his weight from one side to the other.

Kendra shifted, too, then began fussing with her hair.

"Don't think about it, Miles, just start talking. Brainstorm. Whatever comes to mind. Look at her if you need to."

Kendra turned toward him.

Miles made eye contact briefly before looking back at me. "She's pretty—that's the first thing, right?"

"There are no incorrect answers here. Isn't that correct, Kendra?"

"No," she quipped, "but there could definitely be some wrong ones."

"OK, Miles, slide away to the end of the seat and face her."

He did, and he put his elbow on the arm of the love seat and rested his chin on his clenched fist.

She did the same, posing in a mirror image. Their eyes met, now separated by three feet of striped upholstery.

For the first time, with a clear look at her profile, I saw a tired young woman. Much too tired, I thought, for a teenager with the world still waiting for her to arrive.

"Mr. Bohn, looking at your girlfriend, what do you most like about her? What do you most admire about your best friend in the world?"

"Best friend?" He sounded startled.

My heart sank.

Kendra looked like she'd been slapped.

I slid out of my chair and knelt in front of the couple. "Stop thinking, Miles. Just talk."

His eyes went back to hers, but she was studying her hands in her lap. "Look at her," Miles said. "She's the prettiest girl in school, by far."

"She *is* pretty, isn't she? What else?"

"She's a cheerleader."

I withstood the crushing urge to continue steering him, but when he looked down at me for more, I nodded toward her.

"She's smart. She gets straight A's. I've never had straight A's, not once, not even close."

Kendra peeked up at him for the first time. "You're smart, too, Miles."

"Not like you," he argued. "And you're popular, everyone loves you at school."

"They love you, too, right?"

"Wait, Kendra, this isn't about *him* right now. Let Miles talk about *you.*"

"They only like me because I'm with you. And because I play basketball. But you're *everything* at school. You're class president, prom queen, you're pretty much the perfect girlfriend."

Kendra opened her mouth and I stopped the words with a quick, right-hand stop sign. "Are those things you *like* about her, Miles, or just facts about who she is? Like some sort of profile?"

"I like lots more. I like how involved she is, she's all passionate and stuff, and how much she knows about the news, politics, all that."

"You hate politics, Miles."

"No, I don't. Your *dad* hates politics. He hates pretty much everything but basketball."

He stared at her for a moment and a familiar silence filled the room.

"Anything else?"

"It's dumb," Miles said.

"I'm sure it isn't," I said.

"I wish I were more like her."

Kendra covered her mouth with one hand.

"And I guess I like the way she makes me feel."

More silence.

"She makes me feel good."

Kendra slid over next to him and took his hand.

I rose from my knees and backed up to my chair.

"She makes me feel like I matter. Of all the guys in the school, or all the guys in Charlottesville even, she chooses to be *my* girlfriend."

He looked at me for approval and I rewarded him with a subtle, single-fist pump. "Yeah, that's what I like best." Even the air around us could sense his confidence growing. "I like the way she makes me feel."

Kendra looked away from him and appeared to brush away a tear.

"I never feel empty when she's nearby."

I let the moment hang, took a look at the spot where Travis's wheelchair should have been, glanced at my watch, then the alley, then back at the couple.

Kendra rested her head on Miles's shoulder.

"We all deserve to feel that way, don't we, Miles."

"True that, Mr. C. True that."

"Kendra, how long did it take for Miles to change your feelings from insecure to warm and happy?"

She looked at me with the eyes of a wise adult.

"About seventeen seconds."

FIFTEEN

Midnight

THE FRONT DOOR CREAKING OPEN STARTLED ME.

"Cole?"

"Yeah."

"You OK?"

I slapped the spot next to me on the swing. "Join me."

Jade stepped onto the porch, wearing pink sweatpants and a loose-fitting sweatshirt. "It's warm tonight for November," she said, and the fact that I could see her breath proved that everything is relative. She sidled up next to me on the swing and flung her legs over mine. She was wearing one white and one grey sock.

I nodded. "Mmm-hmmm."

"Can't sleep?" Her nose brushed against my right cheek.

I kissed it. "I dunno."

"Don't know if you can't sleep?"

I kicked against the porch floor and the swing began swaying back and forth.

"Cole?"

I kissed her nose again. "I'm all right. Just thinking."

"'Bout?"

"'Bout nothing particular, really."

"It's midnight, sweetheart. No one thinks about nothing at midnight. Especially not men." She ran her index finger along my lower lip and pulled it down. "What's up, Cole Conner?"

I gave the swing another boost. "Just thinking about the kids."

Jade sat up, pivoted on her rear end, and swung her legs around in a wide circle away from me, resting them on the swing bench. Then she placed her head in my lap and put her feet on the swing's armrest. "You knew this session would be tough."

"I guess I did."

"It's just been three Discussions though, right, hon?"

"Just three."

We glided back and forth quietly.

An ambulance passed by without its lights or sirens on.

I stroked Jade's hair and ran thick sections between the fingers of my left hand.

My right hand rested on her belly.

"Did you call Travis?" Jade asked.

"Not yet."

"Are you going to?"

"I can't decide."

I pulled up her shirt two or three inches to expose her belly button. I traced circles around it.

"You could just go by. You have his address, right?"

"I do."

"Or you could just wait and see if he shows up next week."

"I could."

"Or you could have him deported back to Mars."

I tickled her belly.

"Just checking," she teased. "You're zoning me out."

"Never." I ran my finger down the bridge of her nose. "I'm afraid I scared him off for good."

"Because you told the story?"

"Uh-huh. I think it was too early."

"You always tell it early in the Discussions, Cole. That's the point. You *have* to. It's why you're doing all this. It *is* the beginning of it all."

"I know."

"But . . ."

"But maybe I should have been more careful. I don't know much about Travis yet. Maybe it was too much. You should have seen him, Jade. He clammed right up. He looked wounded."

"After Flick died?"

I nodded and resumed tracing the circles on the soft skin across her belly.

"It's a hard thing to hear for the first time, sweetheart, you know that."

I nodded again.

"Maybe he just needed a break," she said. "Or maybe he had something going on? He's a teenager. Don't give up on him. It's just one session."

I leaned down and kissed her forehead. "Do you remember the very first time I told *you* the story?"

"Of course." She sat up, sideways on the swing bench, and tucked her feet under my thigh. "Third date."

"Uh-huh."

"We went for a hike. You packed a junk food picnic, which would have scandalized most girls, but I loved it."

"You're a sucker for Zingers, always have been."

She tugged two fingerfuls of my arm hair. "We sat in a clearing off the trail on a blanket, the one you said you hand-made with your mother. Which could have been a complete line, who knows, but I bought it."

"Well, actually—"

"—and hush," she interrupted. "I don't want to know otherwise." She pulled more hair. "What I do know, and I know this beyond any doubt, is how important it was for you to tell me the story that afternoon. I could see it in your eyes, your mouth. And it just came pouring out of you."

I reached a hand into her lap and wove my fingers into hers.

"It's the story of your life, Cole, and you should never, *ever* regret telling it. It's hard to hear it, of course it is, and it's still incredibly tragic all these years later. Time doesn't change that, but it's a lesson people need to hear. These kids have needed to hear it. And every year when you tell this story to a new group of students, you wonder whether they'll come back for more."

"I know."

"And they always do, Cole. Because something in them says you have more to tell. Something in them says you can change their lives."

I squeezed her hand tighter.

"And you have."

She looked into the darkness. "How long have we been doing this? Ten years? All those summers and falls and all those kids. Some of them have kids of their own now. All of them different people on the last Discussion than the first."

"I like to think so."

"You *know* so, Cole. You're changing lives. I've seen it myself."

"And what if this is the year I can't tell them why they were invited?"

"You won't have to tell them," she whispered. "They'll figure it out on their own."

"And if they don't figure out why they're here?"

"They will."

"How can you be so sure?"

Jade leaned in close enough that our noses touched, and even in the midnight air I could see right through her eyes. "Because," she whispered, "it hasn't been that long since I used to wonder why I was here, too."

I kissed her and she continued, her lips moving across mine as the words escaped. "But if I could figure it out, anyone can."

SIXTEEN

Phone Call

I HADN'T SLEPT WELL.

It was just after eight o'clock on the morning of our fourth Discussion and Jade flicked a ball of Peanut Butter Cap'n Crunch across the table at me. "Wake up, honey."

I rubbed my eyes. "I'm up."

"You're awake, but you most certainly are not *up*." She held her bowl to her mouth and drank the last of the peanut butter–flavored milk. She rinsed her bowl and sat again with a glass of water and her daily vitamins.

"Long night," I said.

She took her pills and threw her head back. "So you're going to wait and see if he shows?"

We'd spent dinner the night before debating—again—whether to call Travis, drive by his home, or wait to see if he arrived with the others. We ate Thai food on the Oriental rug on the floor of the office and studied the single piece of paper

Mr. Buhl had provided with so few details about Travis Nielson. If I'd elected not to call, Jade had even offered to pay the personal visit with me.

"I think I'll wait and see what happens today," I said. "It feels right. I've thought a lot about it overnight."

"Me too." Jade took another drink, set her glass by the sink, and walked out of the kitchen and into our office. A moment later she returned, punching buttons on the cordless phone and looking at a Post-it note stuck to her thumb.

"Who are you—"

She placed the phone in my hand. "It's for you."

"What—"

She whispered, "Come by the store later."

"Wait—"

But she'd already skipped out the side door to her waiting Vespa and Paper Gems.

I put the phone to my ear.

I didn't need to be clairvoyant to know who was on the other end.

"Is anyone there?" The woman's voice was vibrant and loud.

"Hello," I said. "Is this Mrs. Nielson?"

"It is. May I help you?"

"Yes, ma'am, it's Cole Conner."

"Oh goodness, Mr. Conner, thank you for calling. What a nice surprise."

"Thank you, Mrs. Nielson. I apologize for not calling earlier. We missed Travis last week."

Mrs. Nielson hesitated. "Last week?"

"Yes, ma'am, Friday. Our last meeting. We really missed having Travis with us. Will he be joining us today?"

She hesitated again, even longer, and spoke more quietly. "Travis told me you didn't meet last Friday and wouldn't meet at all this week either. He said you had . . . conflicts."

"Hmm. No, Mrs. Nielson, we've had no conflicts."

Mrs. Nielson's prolonged moment of silence actually scared me. "No conflicts?"

"No, ma'am."

"Hmm. Well, sir, he and I are about to have one, I promise you that."

I grimaced. "So he will be here today?"

"Oh yes, Mr. Conner, he will be there."

"Excellent. Tell him I look forward it."

"What time?"

"Five-thirty, and call me Cole, please."

"And you may call me Beth. See you at five-thirty. Good-bye."

I tried to return her good-bye, but she'd already shouted, *"Travis Joseph Nielson!"* and hung up.

I set the phone down and looked at a smiling Cap'n Crunch on the box facing me. "What are you laughing at, Cap'n?"

SEVENTEEN

Halloween

I SPENT THE MORNING AT MY DESK.

I sorted through forms for work, a few prospective client files, and several days of mail. Buried between a Citibank Visa bill and a real estate mailer from Smith Mountain Lake, I found a slick invitation to a release party at Paper Gems. For years, Jade had included our address on her mailing list to get a sense of how long it took for mail to start hitting homes.

I held the glossy postcard advertising a costume party for yet another hot new young adult fantasy series. But like many times before, when I looked at the invitation I really saw a different one, a much older one. It was a twenty-year-old invitation on black-and-red construction paper.

Maddi Denson. Maddi the Bombshell Denson was having a Halloween party that promised to be *Terrrrrifyingly Terrrrrific.* I was invited by a handmade card with jagged trimmed edges made with those fancy scissors and Red Hots glued to the spots where periods should have been. The writing was fancy, too, like calligraphy, except it was actually legible to a boy with the attention span of a SweeTart.

Amazingly, I was only in the sixth grade.

Maddi was in the seventh.

The seventh!

I was decent looking. Average height. Nice hair—according to my mom, anyway. I was smart when I wanted to be. Lazy when I didn't.

But Maddi could have been Miss Teen USA. She was tall. Amazing hair, according to pretty much everyone alive on the planet. She had really white teeth and breath that smelled like Juicy Fruit. I only got close enough to smell it once, but I remember craving the gum as I tried to fall asleep that night. I never told anyone, but I kept an unopened pack in my locker for a month, just in case she ever asked if I had any.

I rushed home to show my mother the invitation.

"An older woman, Cole? I don't know about this." She pretended to fan herself with the card, and a Red Hots went flying.

"Watch it, Mom!" I retrieved it from under a kitchen chair. "So, can I go?"

"I'll talk to Dad."

I knew what *that* meant.

She approved, and Dad probably would, too, but only after a long list of questions about who would be there, where they lived, who their parents were, etc., etc., etc. Dad believed that when it came to friends, there were no secrets.

"Secrets are for eighteen-year-olds," he liked to tease.

Except that he wasn't really teasing.

By sixth grade, I'd learned to expect Dad's odd behavior. I didn't understand it, but it no longer surprised me when he stopped to change tires in the rain, or gave a ride, or bought someone's lunch, or gave up a seat, or hugged a stranger, or punched a man outside an Applebee's for groping a female server.

I remember extraordinarily well the days leading up to the Halloween party at Maddi Denson's house. The fact that I was the only sixth grader invited had spread around the school like lice, and the gossip made me more popular than I'd ever been. Ever *dreamt* of being.

My best friend back then, Zack McKenzi, said he overheard some *eighth* graders talking about me.

Eighth graders!

"Really? No way!" My voice squeaked and I sounded more like a twelve-year-old girl than a twelve-year-old boy. I grabbed the sleeve of his Members Only jacket and yanked him into the boys' room.

"Yeah, Cole, they were. Really. They were standing outside the band room. Swear on a stack of yearbooks."

"Wow wow wow wow wow. Eighth graders?"

"Uh-huh. It's happening, dude. You're going to be popular!"

I floated home that day.

I got invited to a seventh-grader party at Maddi Denson's house. I repeated the words over and over until they'd almost lost their meaning.

Zack heard eighth graders talking about how cool I am. That phrase also took a turn being swished around in my head.

The party was on a Friday night, the night before Halloween, because Maddi's mom didn't want to compete with trick-or-treaters. Most of the kids didn't mind because that meant they'd get even more candy.

I woke up that morning thinking about Maddi.

I ate my Corn Pops thinking about Maddi.

Bus ride? Maddi's smile.

Science? Maddi's Juicy Fruit breath.

By the end of the day I was so dazed and dreamy about Maddi's party that my bus driver had to yell at me, "It's your stop, Cole Conner. Get off or you're walking from the next one."

I wouldn't have cared. I would have walked from Philadelphia if it meant the time passed faster.

When I walked in the door after school, Mom surprised me with an Indiana Jones costume. I had planned on going as a vampire because I already had the teeth and cape and Zack said I looked awesome in it. But when Mom showed me what she'd been making all day, I actually hugged her.

On the table she'd placed a whip she made me promise not to use, khakis, a belt, a tan shirt, and a real fedora that she'd rubbed dirt on to make it looked like it had been on a thousand adventures. It had everything but a gun and holster.

When I came downstairs from changing into it, she was holding a leather jacket that looked exactly like the one Harrison Ford wore in the movie.

"I got this at a thrift store. Do you like it?"

Um, yeah, I thought. I couldn't speak.

"Cole? Are you all right?"

"It's cool, Mom. Really, really cool." I hugged her again.

"You'll be the most handsome sixth grader there," she said.

"I'll be the *only* sixth grader there, Mom."

"Fine then, so you'll be the most handsome young man there in *any* grade."

Mom turned me around and slipped the leather jacket on my shoulders, just like a grown-up, just like I'd seen Dad help her put on her jacket every time they went out.

"Do you think she'll like me?" I asked her.

"Who?"

"Who else, Mom? Maddi."

"Why wouldn't she? You're quite a guy, Cole. You are quite a guy."

We sat at the kitchen table and shared a snack.

Mom reminded me that I was only twelve and just needed to have a good time and not take it quite so seriously.

I reminded her it was my first boy-girl party and I was starting to feel nervous.

Mom said that was perfectly OK.

I didn't say it out loud, but at 5:33 I felt a rush of relief when my father returned home from the radio station. I knew Mom had a property to show that evening and Dad promised to be my ride to and from the party.

"You ready to go, Indy?" Dad said with a goofy smile.

"Sure," I answered nonchalantly, "whenever you're ready."

Ten minutes later, we were in the car making the trip across town to manhood and Maddi Denson's house.

Dad reminded me—again—that I was twelve and wasn't ready to *go with* girls.

I nodded and listened and chewed a piece of Juicy Fruit.

About halfway to Maddi's neighborhood, or so I guessed since I'd never been before, Dad passed a parked sedan with its emergency lights on.

"Let's circle back."

"Dad?"

"Just a second, Cole. It will just take a second."

He pulled a U-turn at the next light, then another to get back on the right side of the divided road, and pulled up behind the car.

"Come on," he said.

I took a quick look at dashboard's digital clock as I stepped out of the car.

We approached from the passenger's side and Dad knocked softly on the window.

The driver, a woman, rolled it down.

From where I stood, a few feet behind Dad and with noisy cars buzzing past us, all I heard was: Engine. Steam. Husband. Boston. Pregnant.

I'd definitely heard enough to worry.

"Dad."

He didn't hear me.

"Dad."

He stood back up and turned around.

"We have to go, Dad."

He held up one finger. "Just another minute." Then he

leaned back into the window and began chatting again with the troubled driver.

A second later, the hood popped up and Dad's head moved from the open window to the engine.

I stood as patiently as a sixth grader waiting to go to a seventh-grader party possibly could.

Soon Dad emerged from behind the hood and went to report back through the window. Another minute later he said, "You can wait in the car, Cole. It's going to be just a few minutes."

A pit began to grow in my stomach.

I returned to our car and breathed a little easier when I realized we weren't officially late yet.

Eight minutes later, when Dad finally returned to the car, we were.

"Hop out, Indy, we need to call a tow truck."

"What?"

"She needs a tow to a shop and no one has called a truck for her yet. There's a pay phone right there." Dad pointed at a phone outside a convenience store less than half a block away.

We jogged there, Dad made the call, Dad said the dispatcher promised to send a truck as soon as possible, and we jogged back.

I dropped into the passenger's seat and Dad returned to the disabled car to update the woman.

Much to my surprise, and I thought, perhaps, as a direct result of fervent prayer, the flashing yellow and white lights of the tow truck arrived sooner than I expected. It felt like a real-life miracle when the lights flickered on the windows as it pulled around us and into position.

Dad again left the car and went to help.

I watched the blocky green minutes flash by on the clock's display.

"Hop in the back, Son," he said through my open window. "We're giving her a ride."

"What?"

"To her home."

"Why, Dad?"

"Because I won't have her ride alone with that driver. She's scared, Cole."

"Where does she live?"

"Not far."

The pit grew bigger and for a while I may have actually stopped breathing. I looked at the time again. "Can't you take me first?"

"Cole, it's not appropriate for me to drive, by myself, a woman to her home. Especially not at night and especially not with her husband out of town."

"But we're late already. Please, Dad."

"Cole, this is the right thing to do. This is our Seventeen Second Miracle for the day. Don't you see it?"

I see something, I thought, *but it's a heck of a lot longer than seventeen seconds.*

I unbuckled, got in the backseat, and watched with horror as the woman walked from her car to ours and took my seat up front.

By the time we pulled into the woman's driveway, we'd already been to an ATM so the woman could get cash to pay the driver, followed the truck to a downtown garage she'd been to before, watched her pay him, listened to her insist over and over and over that we take gas money for our time, listened to her sniffle about her husband's untimely trip to Boston, and driven nearly the length of Albemarle County.

As we pulled out of her driveway, Dad looked at the dashboard clock and simply said, "I'm sorry, Cole."

So I didn't get to Maddi Denson's Terrrrrifyingly Terrrrrific Halloween Party.

So I didn't think it was a miracle.

And I didn't speak to him for three days.

EIGHTEEN

Not Yet

I WAS WAITING AT THE HANDICAPPED SPACE WHEN THEY pulled up.

"Hi, Beth." I shook her hand as Travis made his way off the ramp and toward the store.

"Thanks for calling, Mr. Conner."

"Cole."

"Yes, I'm sorry." She smiled. "What time should I come back for him?"

"Six-thirty?"

"All right then."

I stayed on the sidewalk and watched Beth chase Travis down to say good-bye.

She hugged his shoulders.

He did not hug hers back.

I waited for the van to turn around and head toward the street. I followed well behind Travis, watching him navigate his wheelchair through the store and back to the Reading Corner. I decided to wait another minute before greeting him.

I took my time.

When I finally stepped up to him, I carried two sodas and wore a smile that said that absolutely nothing was out of the ordinary. "Hi, Travis." I handed him a can and leaned against one of the ancient brick walls.

"Hey," he mumbled and took the can.

I popped open my own and enjoyed a sip. "Ah yes, the sweet, sweet taste of caffeine in the afternoon. Keeps me going. Never been a coffee guy, though. Hate the smell." I withstood the urge to see if he was looking at me. Instead, I watched a woman try to find just the right cookbook.

After a few minutes, I glanced at my watch. "I need to run back to Jade's office and get something for today's Discussion. I'll be right back. Miles and Kendra should be here soon." I stepped behind a bookshelf and snuck a peek back at Travis.

He was still sitting, still holding his soda, still looking like he'd rather be anywhere than at Paper Gems.

I walked into Jade's office and retrieved two volumes from the bookshelf. But rather than return immediately, I decided to sit there and wait for Miles and Kendra to arrive.

I don't know why, but Travis needs the time, I thought.

At 5:28, I heard Kendra's voice bubbling as she walked past the office door. I waited one more minute before joining them. When I did, Miles was right where he belonged—on the love seat—and Kendra was standing in front of Travis admiring his latest ball cap, this one bearing the logo of the Washington Capitals hockey team.

"Hi, Mr. Conner," Kendra said.

"Good afternoon, Kendra," I answered. "Hello, Mr. Bohn. You're going to wear my love seat out, you know."

Miles chuckled and gave a "What's up" half-nod.

I pulled my wicker chair to its familiar spot on the floor. "Come on over, Travis. Let's get started."

He rolled into place, completing the circle, but had yet to make eye contact.

"So," I began, "everyone have a good weekend?"

"I did," Kendra chirped first.

"OK, then tell us one nice thing that happened to you since we last met."

"Easy," she said. "I got into the school yesterday and started rearranging the Student Council office. When I took a break, Dad let me shoot around in the gym. He never does that. He even played H-O-R-S-E with me. I beat him with a left-handed layup."

"Really?" Miles asked.

"Uh-huh. Then he went back to the coaches' office and I totally organized the SCA stuff. I got permission to put up a new message board. Also cleaned up some old folders on the SCA laptop."

"Sounds productive," I said.

"I know, right?"

"Well-done. How about you, Travis? Anything good happen to you this week?"

"Uh-uh."

"Nothing?"

He shook his head.

"Something good must have happened. I'll come back to you." I turned to Miles and prayed he'd have a long enough answer for Travis to make something up, if nothing else. "Miles?"

"I made fifty consecutive free throws last Friday at practice."

"That's fantastic, Miles. Congratulations. That's really something, a fine achievement indeed. But that's something good you made happen, right? What about something good just happening to you?"

"Like, by luck?"

"No, not necessarily. Did anyone do something good for you? Or to you?"

"Kendra's dad stood under the basket and fed the ball back to me. Does that count?"

I laughed. "Sure, today we'll count it."

I held my breath and looked at Travis. "All right, Mr. Nielson. You're up."

He shrugged.

"Just think back on the last few days. Something good must have happened. Did anyone do anything nice for you? Your mother? Father?"

"My father is in jail."

"Oh, I'm sorry, Travis. I had no idea. What about your mother? Maybe a friend?"

He thought for a moment and then tapped the bill of his hat. "My hat."

"Excuse me?"

"Kendra said she liked my new hat."

I looked at her and she flashed him a wide, genuine smile.

"You're welcome, Travis," she said.

I could have hugged her. "That's excellent. Just excellent. That's a *great* example."

Travis looked up at me for the first time that day. He didn't grin, wink, or thank me. Just a quick look in my eyes. It was a start.

"So you all remember that last week I told you the most important story of our time together. It's really one of the most important stories of my life, and I wasn't even there. I don't want to dwell on the sadness of Flick's death, but I want to know what you felt in the hours and days after our Discussion."

I looked at Kendra.

She was silent.

Miles was already in his "chill" position. Legs outstretched. Staring up. Head leaned back on the top of the seat.

"You know," I pressed ahead, "I was pretty down that afternoon after you all left. And I've lost count of how many times I've told or thought about that story and those seventeen seconds."

Quiet.

"What I'm saying is that it's completely natural to feel sorrow for something you didn't experience yourself. If any of you told me you went home and pushed Flick completely out of your mind, that you didn't spend a single moment thinking of how her passing affected her sister and mother, not to mention my father, I'd be very worried. We're pre-built to feel sympathy, at least we should be."

I took a breath and waited.

I looked at Kendra.

Kendra looked at Travis.

Travis looked at the ground.

"I was sluggish," Miles finally said.

I nearly fell from my chair. "Sluggish?"

"Yeah. I had practice that evening and I was slow. I felt kinda out of it. Sad, you know, just not really myself, I guess. Hearing it all, the little girl dying, it was a lot to hear. At practice, Coach said my feet looked like they were stuck in mud. I couldn't even make free throws. Honestly I didn't want to be there at all."

I glanced at Travis and Kendra. Both were wide-eyed and watching Miles with curiosity and concern.

Travis more of the former.

Kendra the latter.

Miles must have sensed the quiet had grown uncomfortably long, because he looked right at me and said, "Coach said I wasn't hydrating. He yelled at me and made me drink so much water I almost wet my pants."

Travis stifled a laugh.

Kendra shook her head and covered her face.

"And there he is, folks," I teased.

Miles smiled.

"I'm thankful you didn't have any bladder-control issues, Miles."

"Me too."

We made small talk for a few minutes about Miles, basketball, the new gym, conditioning, and cheerleaders.

Then Kendra redirected us. "I wanted to give him a hug."

"Who?" I asked, though we weren't so far from the Discussion that I really wondered.

"Your dad. Rex, right?"

"Yes."

"I wanted to just hug him. I wanted to tell him it wasn't his fault."

"Is that what you felt when you left that day?"

"Not just that day, Mr. Conner. Every day since then. I wanted to tell you how much I'd been thinking about it last week, but we didn't get a chance."

I couldn't tell where Travis was looking, or whether he was still engaged in the Discussion at all, but I hoped he was.

"I'm glad, Kendra."

"Glad?"

"Not glad. More like pleased. Pleased the moment affected you. I know my father would be honored that you felt for him."

"I just want to hug him," she said again. "I wish he were here."

"Me too, Kendra."

We looked at each other and I smiled, knowing how much my father would have appreciated a young woman like Kendra.

The floor suddenly creaked as Travis rolled forward an inch or two and then back.

"Travis? You want to share how you felt last week?"

Again he rolled forward and back.

"Travis?"

He took his Capitals cap off and rubbed his buzzed head.

"Take your time," I said.

His eyes followed a loud motorcycle as it passed down Main Street. It was only in view for a second, but Travis seemed to track the sound for a mile. "Nah," he finally said.

"You sure?"

He put his cap back on, twisted it slightly off center, cracked his knuckles, and shook his head at me.

Not yet, I thought. *Not yet.*

NINETEEN

Journals

"I'D LIKE TO SHARE SOMETHING ELSE WITH YOU THIS WEEK."

I reached under my chair and picked up my father's journal.

All eyes were fixed on the leather-bound, eight-by-ten-inch book.

"This belonged to my father. It's his journal. He had others when this one filled up, but this was the very first. He gave it to me when I started leading these Discussions." I opened it to a random entry, roughly in the middle, and turned it around so everyone could see.

Travis moved a little closer.

"After Flick's drowning in 1970, my father entered a very dark place. You already know that he even tried to commit suicide. He was lost. And despite Sparks staying with him, it was a lonely time for my father. Have any of you ever felt anything close to that?"

Miles and Kendra shook their heads at me.

Travis shrugged.

"One day something happened. Something that opened the shades just enough for him to see that there was, in fact, still light outside his darkening world."

I handed the journal to Travis on my left. "Have a look, pass it around."

I watched as he opened it and turned the delicate pages, as if handling a thousand-year-old Bible.

"One Sunday my father went walking to this very down-town mall. Many of the shops were closed and only a handful of other pedestrians were out and about. He was alone . . .

"Sparks, still technically his girlfriend at the time though they didn't spend as much time together as they once had, was out of town for the weekend with her mother. They were, quite naturally, still grieving, and my dad hadn't been invited on any trips with the family since the drowning . . .

"On this Sunday afternoon, feeling even more alone than usual, Dad excused himself to the restroom during church and slipped out the back door. A short walk later and he was sitting on an outside bench in front of Woolworth's, a store that's been gone for a long, long time."

"I've heard of Woolworth's," Kendra said. "My mom worked there when she was a kid. She said it was like an old-timers' Wal-Mart."

"That's pretty close," I said. "And right in front of Wool-worth's there was a bench. From that bench, my father watched an older woman come out of the front door, catch her purse strap on the handle, briefly lose her balance, and spill both her purse and a shopping bag all over the brick sidewalk . . .

"She bent over to retrieve her things, and, without thinking, Dad hopped off the bench and insisted she stand back up. He got on all fours and gathered the items. The last thing he'd picked up was a tan spiral notebook with a small pencil tucked into the wire at the top. He waited patiently for her to get the rest of her belongings settled back into both her purse and the shopping bag. When she finally took the notebook from him, she asked, 'May I know your name?'

" 'Rex Conner.'

" 'Lovely name. You have just made my journal, Mr. Conner.'

" 'Huh?'

" 'That notebook you are holding. Every time someone special happens to me, I put it in there to remember.'

" 'Oh,' Dad answered.

"The woman then walked to the bench my father had been parked on and began writing. After a few lines, she looked at my father and asked, 'Do you know the date today, young man?'

"He answered and she resumed writing. After another few lines she paused, looked my father in the eyes, and said, 'Ten years ago, when my husband was still alive, he would have been the one to pick up my things for me. So I thank you, Rex Conner, for helping me today. And I think he would want to thank you, too.'

"They chatted for another few minutes and the woman moved on. He said he watched her walk all the way up the mall and down a side street until all he could see was the space on the bench next to him where she'd sat. He remained still, thinking about her for the longest time. At some point he wandered back to church. Later that afternoon, he shared the story with his mother and stepfather. And the next afternoon when Dad got home from school, this exact journal was sitting on his bed, wrapped in a purple bow with a brand-new pen."

My hand moved across the worn cover as I continued. "Dad began to write down things that made him happy, things that gave him hope. Most of those things involved the feelings of gratitude that come from being served. He wrote a lot about what others did for him. He wrote less about what he did for others, but I know a lot about that part of him, too."

I reached under the chair and pulled out another journal. "When Sparks saw what a change keeping a journal made in Dad's life, she began to keep one, too. She wrote about her life but also his descriptions of his experiences. Dad was modest in his entries, Sparks was accurate. Between the two, I have a precious picture and priceless set of memories of my father."

I read them the first entry out of each book.

❧

TWENTY

Rex's Journal

December 18, 1970

This is my first entry in the journal Mom bought me last week.

She really liked the story about the lady by Woolworth's and thinks I should do a journal also.

I'm doing it because it will make Mom happy. She has not acted happy much at all this year.

It is Friday and today someone did something nice for me.

After school in the parking lot Jessica Earnhardt told me she liked my poem from English class today. She's never spoken to me this year. Or I don't remember anyway if she did.

She was the only one to tell me they liked it and it made me feel good.

Maybe this is not what the lady on the mall meant to write about. I don't know. But I promised Mom I would use it.

So this is my first entry.

Jessica Earnhardt said she liked my poem.

TWENTY-ONE

Sparks's Journal

December 25, 1970

Merry Christmas! When I opened the art kit that included this little notebook, I considered it a sign that I should start keeping a journal like Rex's. I still have my diary but that's for me. This is for Rex to have one day. I don't know how long we will be close but I know we'll always be friends.

He told me he's going to use his journal to remember the good things that happen to him. Half the stuff he's told me so far is about things he's done for other people. When he told about the lady at Woolworth's, he talked about how cool the journal idea was but he didn't write anything down about how he helped her put her purse and shopping bag back together.

I'm going to write down good things that happen to me and Rex and also try to write the stories he tells me but is too shy to put in his own journal.

TWENTY-TWO

Mall Walker

DEATH, TAXES, AND MALL WALKERS.

They are universal. Unavoidable.

Fashion Square Mall in Charlottesville is no different than any mall in America. During the morning hours, often when the stores are still dark and lonely, hiding behind silver metal grates that disappear into the ceiling, the walkers are pumping their arms and circling the mall perimeter.

Some push strollers.

Some push gossip.

The morning after our fourth conversation, I found myself sitting in the center of the mall watching the mall walkers scamper along the storefronts in their active leisure wear, chatting and dodging janitors doing the final checkups before the stores and jewelry and pretzel kiosks opened.

I've been there before when I needed a reminder of why the miracles matter. It is, undoubtedly, one of the easiest places to perform a Seventeen Second Miracle. I must have seen Dad perform at least one on every single trip to every single shopping center we ever visited.

But his hometown mall was always his favorite. Dad called Fashion Square Mall a *rookie's paradise.*

"You can't swing and miss here, Cole. It's like a batting cage that serves up pitches bigger than a beach ball. You can hit a beach ball, right, Cole?"

He used to say this to me in the car as we came to a stop in a parking spot as far from the door as possible.

"Yes, Dad, but do we have to park back here?"

"Of course we do."

"Why? There are spaces closer."

"Son, those spaces are for people who need them more."

"They're not handicapped spaces, Dad."

"That doesn't matter, Cole. Someone will come today with a baby in a stroller or leave with an armful of bags. Because we parked back here, they'll get to park closer."

"Dad, we're past even the employee parking spots."

"So?"

"So I can barely even see the entrance from here."

The script usually ended there when Dad put his arm around me. I knew if I pushed the discussion, it would end like this:

"You have legs?"

"Yes, Dad."

"They working all right?"

"Yes, Dad."

"You got anything heavy in your arms?"

"No, Dad."

"You in a hurry?"

"You know I'm not."

"Then why not take a few extra steps simply because you can, and let others take a few less."

I've always believed if you only added up the walking we did between our car and the mall, our car and the church, our car and Wal-Mart, and our car and Kroger, we could have walked from Charlottesville to San Francisco.

Sitting in a soft chair by Starbucks in the center of the mall that day, I made a mental note that if Travis returned to the Discussions, I'd tell that story with even more sensitivity than usual.

"May I?" A woman approached and motioned to another brown leather chair very close to mine and at a slight angle. The armrests nearly touched at their ends.

"Of course," I answered.

The woman, probably in her fifties, plopped into the chair and immediately began digging through her purse on her lap. She wore black walking shoes, white socks, shiny blue exercise pants with zippers on the sides of the legs, and a matching workout jacket zipped halfway up. I noticed that her jacket had the name *Freakley* embroidered on the chest.

After rummaging through her purse for an awkward five minutes, she turned toward me and sighed.

"Couldn't find it?" I asked.

" 'Fraid not."

"I'm sorry about that."

"Why would you be?"

"Good point."

She looked back at her purse and took another tour of every pocket and pouch. "It was here this morning. I put it in. I know I did."

"Can I help?" I offered.

She replied by looking up at me, furrowing her brow, and resuming the purse pillage.

A gaggle of mall walkers, larger than most, passed by us on the other side of the mall's center atrium. The more I watched them, the more they looked like Canadian geese skirting the edge of a lake.

"They look like geese, don't they?"

The woman ignored me, or at least gave the undeniable impression she did.

More awkward silence followed.

Then more.

"Oh, look." I pointed at a woman pushing a jogging stroller and joining the walkers from behind. "They picked up a chick."

Nothing.

Then more nothing, and I eventually lost my gaze in the food court to my left.

A cry turned my attention back to her. I suppose it wasn't so much a cry as it was a snort, but when I looked at her, she was, in fact, wiping at the corners of both eyes with both thumbs.

"Ma'am?"

No answer.

"Are you OK?"

Nothing.

I left the chairs and bought a bottle of water from Starbucks. "Here," I said when I returned, offering it to her.

She took it, opened it, took a long drink, placed the bottle on the floor between our seats, and nodded what I could only read as a *Thank you*.

I nodded back what I hoped she recognized as a *You're very welcome*.

We sat for a while and watched as the gaggle returned from the Sears end of the mall, made a loop past Belk, and disappeared into the long end of the cross-shaped Fashion Square.

"They're really *flying* today, aren't they?" I said as the last straggler caught up to the group.

I turned to look at the woman again when she didn't answer.

The corners of her mouth turned up just a few degrees into a very subtle smile. "That was awful," she said.

"Awful?"

"The chick was one better, if I'm being frank."

"You be Frank. I'll be Cole." I reached out to shake her hand. "Or are you . . . Freakley?"

She shook my hand and glanced at her jacket. "That's my last name. It's Ann Freakley," she said. "But my friends call me Helga."

"You're kidding."

"About what?" she answered in mock offense.

"Helga?"

At last she displayed the smile I'd been waiting for. "It's true, young man. It's my nickname."

I pursed my lips. "With all due respect—Helga?"

She winked approval at my using the name.

"Helga? Really? Helga? When they were picking nicknames for you, you didn't consider something more . . . more . . ."

"Delicate?" She saved me.

"Exactly. Anna Banana, something like that. It's not too late, you know."

She laughed. "Oh yes, son, I think so. I'm afraid Helga it is."

We continued making small talk as the seconds ticked by. She was originally from Baker City, Oregon. Married a salesman. Moved to Crozet. Earned her nickname in a bowling league. Averaged just shy of 200 and once bowled a 269 at a surprise birthday party when pregnant.

When the mall walkers reappeared to begin another lap, I watched as she once again began searching through her purse.

"Helga, may I ask what you're searching for with such intensity? Can I help?"

She looked at me with heavy eyes. "My husband. I have a picture of him, a small one, in a locket, but it's so small and the chain is gone. It's settled in here some . . ."

And with that thought hanging unfinished on her lips, she pulled a gold locket, no bigger than a quarter and almost as thin, from the bottom of her purse. She opened it and handed it across the armrests to me.

I held it with my thumb and index finger. "A handsome man," I said.

"Yes, he was."

"He's gone?"

She nodded.

"I'm sorry, Helga."

"So am I."

I handed the locket back to her and we sat in silence.

"We used to be walkers, too," she said.

"Excuse me?"

"Stu and I. We walked here all the time."

I smiled, first at her, then at the gaggle as it passed us yet again.

"It's been a while?" I posed.

"Since?"

"Since you walked."

"It has."

"May I ask when your husband died?"

She looked down at the locket. "Thirty-eight days ago."

I am certain—as certain as death, taxes, and mall walkers—that what happened next was exactly what my father would have done. But what made the lump form in my throat was that I didn't do it for him; I did it for her.

I stood up and held out my hand, palm exposed.

She took it and I softly tugged her out of the chair and to her feet.

She slung her purse over her shoulder.

I extended my elbow and she looped her arm through mine.

Then we walked.

TWENTY-THREE

Dinner

I PICKED UP MOM AT 6:30.

Jade was working late, hosting a reading and signing for a novelist from the Shenandoah Valley. I usually attend those sorts of events at Paper Gems, but Jade waved me off that morning over breakfast.

"It's fine if you skip this one, babe. This guy's not exactly writing your kind of books," she said.

"No pictures?"

"Exactly."

"Scratch-and-sniff panels?"

"None, sorry."

So instead, Jade suggested I take my mother to dinner, something we hadn't done in far too long.

Not surprisingly, Mom loved the idea.

"Look at you, Cole," Mother said as I opened the passenger

door and waited for her to climb in the car. "All dapper and well dressed. I would have worn something else if I'd known."

I didn't tell her I'd had a client meeting late that afternoon and gone straight to her townhouse on Pantops Mountain, just outside the Charlottesville city limits. "I'll do anything to impress a girl, you know that."

"Yes, I do," she said as I slammed the door shut.

We drove to a steakhouse she and Dad used to enjoy and were seated in less than a minute. It was slow, even for a weeknight.

For the first ten minutes, we played catch-up.

Mom had added another day per week to her volunteer commitment at the senior center.

My office manager convinced me to add another employee to the payroll at my financial services firm.

Mom painted her sunroom that past weekend—again. "I'll find the right color." She sighed. "One of these days."

"You don't like the yellow?"

"Actually, it's light blue."

"Since when?"

"Since the burgundy."

"Oh my. Time to ground you from Sherwin-Williams?"

"I know, dear. I have a paint problem."

"Well, Mom, admitting it is the first step."

We laughed and I wished it hadn't been so long since just the two of us had shared a date night.

Mom had been in the townhouse on Pantops for three years. She and Dad had bought it when his condition worsened more rapidly than the doctor predicted and their old house in nearby Keswick proved to be too much home and too much worry.

But if guests didn't know better, they wouldn't know Dad was gone. The walls and shelves proudly and prominently proclaimed: *I'm still here.*

Mom wouldn't have it any other way.

Dad was as much a part of our lives now as when he did more than just smile from photos in expensive frames.

"How are they going?" Mom asked as the waiter placed beer-battered onion rings on the table between us.

"How's what going?"

"You know what. The Discussions."

"Oh, those." I dipped an onion ring in the accompanying spicy sauce. "They're OK."

"Just OK?"

Mother always knew more than she let on. As a child, I learned to be careful with my version of the truth, because I knew that more often than not she already knew the answers to the questions she was asking. Or at least enough to send me to my room for a couple of hours.

"It's been a struggle at times," I admitted.

Mother already knew some of the details. She'd been to Sunday dinner twice since this season's Discussions had started, and spoke to Jade more often than she did to me. So she already knew full well that it was a smaller-than-usual group, that one student was in a wheelchair, and that only one—Kendra—ever had much to say.

"Do they know yet?" Mom asked.

"Know what?"

"Why they were invited."

"No."

"Do you?"

"Not a clue."

I told her about the time Travis didn't come, and the Discussion I had had with Kendra and Miles in his absence. "They're just so young to be so serious."

Mom took a drink of her ice water, then asked, "Are they as serious as it seems?"

"I don't follow you."

"You know young romance, Cole. They're all Romeo and Juliet until the boy talks to another girl or the girl giggles too loud at some other boy's joke. Then what seemed like true love ends as quickly as it started."

"I don't know, Mom. I really don't. They do seem . . . I don't know . . . mature. Sometimes they seem like a married couple already."

Mom reminisced about her tumultuous romance with Dad.

I reminisced about my courtship with Jade.

Our server came with my New York strip and Mom's lime chicken and rice.

"Tell me about the other boy."

"Travis. He's even harder to read. He's got a gentle quality, Mom, something very appealing. But he's got things going on inside that I can't quite get to."

"How many times have you met?"

"Four. He's been to three."

"And how many are left?"

"Six or seven." If this had been a skit, I could have delivered her next line for her.

"You have plenty of time left, Cole."

"I know, Mom."

"Be patient, Son. You know as well as anyone these lessons take time. You'll figure it out. So will they."

I picked at my baked potato. "I just want the best this year."

"Best?" she asked.

"Best experience."

"For whom? You or the kids?"

"All of us."

She smiled. "You're just like your father, you know that?" Then she reached across and took one of my hands in both of hers. "Cole, be patient. Remember what Dad used to say?"

I did, but I let her say it anyway, and I knew she was right before the words ever crossed the table.

"Just because the lessons are *about* the Seventeen Second Miracle, doesn't mean we learn them that fast."

An hour passed in old robe—comfortable conversation about Jade, the bookstore, her neighborhood Home Owners Association, local politics, and memories of Dad.

We fought over the check, a ritual whenever we ate and a ritual that always ended with me paying.

I drove her home and walked her to the door.

We shared a long hug and I walked back to my car, knowing she would still be standing outside until I was safely buckled and on my way.

I stopped just before dipping my head into the car. "Mom?"

"Yes, dear."

"Will you come to the next Discussion?"

"Can I tell them about me?"

I thought about it for a minute and decided that it was about the right time. "Sure."

"Good. See you, what, tomorrow?"

"Tomorrow."

TWENTY-FOUR

Baby Books

THE LIGHTS WERE STILL ON.

The neighboring businesses were all closed and there was plenty of parking on the street near Paper Gems, a rare luxury in a downtown with precious little off-street parking.

The store's front door was locked. I peered in the window but couldn't spot anyone up front.

I used my key and called loudly as I stepped in, "It's the Homicide Detective, Special Reindeer Victims' Unit, hello?"

No reply.

"It's the po po, anyone here?"

I passed a red-and-green-skirted banquet table holding leftover sugar cookies and a few dirty plastic cups. Some of the chairs had been folded up; others remained in place. The wooden, unbalanced lectern stood in its usual spot.

"Jade?" I called.

"Back here." Her voice told me I wouldn't need to see her eyes to know she'd been crying.

I found her in the corner of the reference section in an oversized canvas beanbag.

"Hey you," I said as I tossed my sport coat over a circular book rack.

Jade clutched an obviously used Kleenex.

"Sweetheart?" I cozied into the beanbag next to her and picked up a book off her lap: *What to Expect When You're Expecting.*

"It's the updated version." She sniffled.

"Just come out?"

"Uh-huh." She motioned toward three more copies just like it on a shelf to her right.

"I'm sorry, darling."

She wiped her nose. "I'm fine. Just came back to shelve a couple of deliveries today and this was in it. I'm fine, really."

"Are you convincing me or you?" I freed a few stray strands of hair that had gotten stuck in the dried tears on her cheek.

"I'm fine," she repeated.

I reached over her on one knee and slid the book onto the shelf next to the others.

"You know these books are a scam, right? What do you really need to know? When a man and a woman love each other very much, they wrestle, then boom, things happen, babies are made, the babies cook, they come out, they talk back, they want the car keys. I mean, seriously, I could write one of those books."

Jade gave a quick courtesy chuckle, leaned into me, and put her head on my chest.

"I'm sorry, Jade. Just trying to help."

"I know you are." She pulled gently down on my tie and pretended to strangle me with the knot.

"There's always the—"

"Shhh." She put a finger over my lips. "Just listen."

"To what?"

"The books."

It wasn't the first time we'd sat in the stillness of Paper Gems. The bookstore had been a place of refuge, first for Jade and then for both of us.

It caught Jade's tears when her mother had finally succumbed to diabetes.

It brought peace when Jade was so shaken by a dog attack that she wouldn't ride her Vespa or walk downtown for a month. The bite healed much more quickly than her nerves.

Paper Gems had hosted birthday parties, candlelit dinners, and a surprise anniversary present for me: a visit and chat from local author John Grisham.

It also hosted two baby showers.

Neither was for her.

Jade and I had tried for a baby almost immediately after getting married and settling into our routine in Northern Virginia. But the stress of long commutes and longer days wasn't conducive, Jade thought, to getting pregnant. It was another of the reasons we had moved south to Charlottesville. But after two miscarriages and dozens of appointments with nearly as many specialists, we learned our problem had less to do with life's natural anxieties and more to do with the tumors in her uterus.

"The bad news," the doctor said, "is that your uterus is lined with fibroids. Tumors. The good news is that they're benign, as is most commonly the case."

He went on to explain that Jade had a rather common ailment in an uncommon way. She had developed the tiny tumors on the walls of her uterus much younger than most women, and had more than he'd ever seen before.

"Jade, I wish the news were better. But you will never conceive a child. I am terribly sorry. The tumors will only grow. The recommended course is a hysterectomy."

He could have stabbed her in the belly and caused less pain.

Even before the surgery I offered to begin looking into adoption, but Jade was reluctant. "If God wanted us to have a baby, he would have sent a baby, not tumors."

We'd never been regular churchgoers, and after the realization she'd never be a mother, I suspected we'd go even less frequently.

I was right.

We didn't visit the church again until after her mother died.

Jade hadn't necessarily become bitter. She was brittle.

She wasn't angry with God. She was defeated.

"I won't feel sorry for myself and blame God. I won't. I'll just live a different life than the one I dreamt of."

It didn't matter how many times I'd heard the words, the look on her face when we passed strollers in the grocery store or heard a baby cry in the next aisle convinced me she still ached for a child of her own.

Sitting on a beanbag chair on the floor of Paper Gems that night, I was reminded yet again how much we'd changed together, and how much we owed to her mother and my father.

TWENTY-FIVE

The Guest

MOTHER WAS ALREADY AT PAPER GEMS WHEN I GOT THERE at five o'clock.

"You didn't come at all last year, did you?" I asked.

"I don't think so, no. Was it '08 that the boy from England was in the group?"

"Good memory." I sat next to her in my usual spot. "His name was Liam and he still e-mails me every month or two. He's at Georgetown."

"How many of these kids are like that?" she asked as she brought a cup of tea to her mouth to cool it with a long breath.

"Like what?"

"Have kept in contact."

"Quite a few," I admitted as I dragged a chair over for her to join the circle when the kids arrived. "But that particular group two years ago, well, they were a good bunch."

She daintily dabbed a drop of tea from the corner of her

mouth. "They've all been good groups, haven't they?" It felt less like a question and more like a reminder.

"It's true," I conceded. "Each is just different. This one feels like it's coming together more slowly, for some reason. But I do enjoy their company."

We changed topics long enough to discuss Dad, a few of her new listings, Jade, and at what point I'd get Mom's amended tax return done.

As 5:30 approached, I guided us back to the Discussions. "Anything more you want to know about the kids?"

"Not really. Let's just chitchat with them. Let me share a little of Dad. See where it goes."

Mother had been a presence at the Discussions before. Not just two years earlier, but anytime I felt stymied or thought the kids would benefit from her angle. And, occasionally, she'd come just because she wanted to be around them. She came almost every week one summer early on.

Miles and Kendra arrived a few minutes after 5:30.

Before the couple could sit, I waved Mother over to say hello. "This is my mother, Oakley Conner."

Both Miles and Kendra shook her hand politely.

"It's nice to meet you, Mrs. Conner," Kendra said.

Miles nodded in agreement and plopped into his customary seat.

Mother returned the pleasantries and complimented Kendra's new shoes. Then she looked at Miles and admired his iPhone. "Isn't that the best invention ever?"

"You have one?" Miles asked.

"No, I have *two*. I bought the first gen the day it came out, then I replaced it with a 3G. I use the old one as an iPod now."

Miles's mouth hung open. "That's friggin' awesome."

Mother retrieved her phone from her purse. "You have the *Christmas Jars* app?" she asked.

I winked at Kendra as her boyfriend and my mother glided into a conversation comparing applications and ringtones.

At 5:40, Travis arrived in usual fashion. He rolled through the store, was introduced to my mother, and half-smiled as he passed by Kendra. He did a quick 180-spin on two wheels and settled into place.

I began with, "Welcome, everyone, nice to have you back."

That was met with:

"Yeah."

"Of course."

"Sure thing."

I grabbed dramatically onto the armrests of my chair and shook it. "Easy kids. Don't let your excitement disturb the customers."

They laughed. Even Travis didn't try to stifle a chuckle.

"I want to talk about the journals again, then you can grill my mother with some questions. But first, around the room we go, tell us one nice thing done to you this week."

"Can I start?" Mother asked.

"Why not?"

"A very handsome man bought me dinner at my favorite place." She batted her eyelashes at Kendra.

"Does Mrs. Conner have a man?" Kendra teased.

"Several," Mom teased back. "But this time your distinguished lecturer here was my date."

"All right, troublemakers, don't make me send the new kid to the principal's office . . . Miles, how about you?"

"Can I pass?"

"For the day?"

"Just for a minute."

"Hmmm, request granted. Kendra?"

"Easy for me. Mrs. Taylor, the SCA advisor, said I could call her Heidi when the other students weren't around."

Miles laughed. And not *with* her, it seemed, but *at* her.

"That's not bad," I admitted. "I can see why you thought that was a nice thing done to you, a little miracle in your life, but can you think of something beyond SCA? Beyond school?"

She crossed her legs and leaned back in the love seat. "Can I pass?"

"For—"

"—for just a minute," she interrupted.

"Travis Nielson. You're my only hope. What do you have for us?"

He started fidgeting with the wheels on his chair again. "Nothin' really."

"Come on, Travis, I know something, *something* nice was done for you this week. It's been two days since you sat here with me and answered the same question. In two days *something* good had to have happened to you. Brainstorm out loud if you need to."

His eyes shifted from Miles to Kendra, then to mine for an instant, then back to Kendra. "Do I have to say it?"

"I'd really like you to. Yes. It's a good exercise. I promise."

His eyes narrowed and I am convinced they looked in mine and said, *You promise you won't call my mom again?*

"OK, there was one thing," he said and I think he peeked at my mother. "The rehab center is gonna get me a new chair."

"That's great, Travis. Now nobody will be able to keep up with you."

"Yeah, something like that," he replied.

"Miles," I said with some force, mostly to get the attention back off of Travis. "Round two for you."

"I got one." He pulled something from his wallet. "A gas card."

"Um, gas card?"

"Yeah, from my mom, so I don't have bug her for money all the time. I can buy whatever I want on it at the gas station."

"Cool," Travis said.

Miles looked at me. "That's something nice, right?"

I moved my hands up and down, as if weighing something on an invisible scale. "Sort of, yes. I suppose so. The spirit of it is certainly there."

He beamed.

"Well-done. And to you again, Kendra."

"I came up with something, but it's probably not what you're looking for, Mr. Conner."

"Try me."

"This morning my dad said something to my mother about me and I was standing right there."

Uh-oh, I thought.

"He said he thought I'd be a good mother one day, if I wanted to be."

Perfect.

"Is that OK?"

"That's wonderful, Kendra. Did it make you feel good?"

"Yeah."

"Then it was perfect," I said.

As I reached down to pick up my father's journal, Kendra stood and asked, "Do you have a restroom?"

My mother volunteered to show her the way.

While they were gone, Miles bragged about the satellite radio he'd installed in his Saab.

When they returned, Kendra wore a big grin and Mom a sly smile. I slid to the edge of my chair and held up the journal in front of my chest.

"Travis, what do we know about this journal so far?"

"It was your old man's."

"Yes, good. Miles, what else?"

"He wrote in it."

"Geniuses, both of you. Kendra, help them out."

"It's not a regular journal or diary?"

"Go on," I offered.

"It was just for service," Kendra answered. "Like when someone did something kind for him. Like the time the girl said she liked his poem."

Mother turned to me. "That's one my favorites," she said, and put both hands on her heart.

"Me too. But there's one more important thing. And we

didn't really discuss it, but it's perhaps the most essential element of the journals."

My mother raised her hand.

Miles, Kendra, and Travis all snickered.

"Yes, ma'am," I said.

"I bet I know. May I?" She didn't wait for an answer. "What makes my Rex's journals so special is that he never wrote things *he* did for other people. He only wrote things other people did for *him*."

"Why?" The question came from Miles.

"The journal is a reminder, Miles. It's a reminder of how blessed he'd been by others. It wasn't some kind of resume of all the things he'd done for other people. That was never the point. That would have felt presumptuous, as if he'd wanted credit."

"Didn't he?" Kendra wondered.

"Not at all. He did those things, performed those miracles, for the well-being of the people he served."

"And in the meantime . . ." I added.

"And in the meantime he grew," she continued. "That's part of the wonder of the miracles. The more you serve others, the more you're really serving yourself."

The kids looked equally confused.

"Think of it this way," she said. "Think of it as a bank account with a huge balance. You spend and spend, but the more you spend, the more money is in your account. Every time you go back to the bank, your balance has grown."

Travis grunted. "That's messed up."

"How so?" I asked.

"Real life isn't like that. You don't get more cash just because you blow more money."

Mother began flipping pages in the journal. "May I read something to you?"

"Yeah."

"Of course."

"Sure thing."

TWENTY-SIX

Rex's Journal

June 12, 1971

I don't know how I did it, but I just survived high school. Today was graduation. During the program something happened that Sparks said should go in my journal. She's says she's keeping one now, too. Got it last Christmas. It bothers me a little that she can read mine but she won't let me see hers. Girls.

So every year the students vote on one cool teacher to help hand out diplomas. They get to stand by Principal Shaffer and shake your hand when you come up.

This year we voted on H.B. He's a track coach. He wins the vote a lot of years because he's so many kids' favorite.

I didn't know him very well except that he taught my driver's ed class last year. He said hi to me a lot in the hallways, and sometimes he stopped to ask how I was doing, but we were not really good friends. He stopped a lot of kids to say hi.

When they called my name I walked across the stage, but when I got to H.B. he didn't shake my hand. He hugged me instead. When I let go he grabbed me again and said something in my ear: "I knew you could do it, Rex. You are an amazing young man."

I couldn't believe it. Why would he say that? We didn't know each other very good at all.

After they gave out all the diplomas, Principal Shaffer stood back up and made an announcement. He said he had a special surprise. H.B. was going to retire that year, no one in the school but Principal Shaffer and a couple others in the office knew. And because he'd been so important to the school for so long (he's a pretty old guy), he was asked to speak. Principal Shaffer said that maybe no teacher had given the school so much for so long.

When H.B. got to the mic, he started to cry right off the bat. He tried to talk, and he started to thank everyone for everything they'd done for him at AHS. But he just started to cry again. He coughed and choked and said how much he would miss the school and the students. He said he could never repay the other teachers or the kids for everything they'd done for him.

Then out of nowhere some seniors in the front row got up and walked toward the stage. Then some others followed. Sparks went too. I was one of the last.

We walked up the steps and we gathered around H.B. and filled the whole stage. There was 150 of us, maybe more, all crowded around the stage and hanging off the sides. Some of the other people sitting up there hopped off to give more room. Kids were on chairs and waving their arms. All to support H.B.

Then someone started chanting, "Thank you, H.B.! Thank you, H.B.! Thank you, H.B.!" Kinda like a cheerleader chant.

Soon the entire place was chanting along. Moms and dads and friends. Other teachers. Even kids.

H.B. ended up on some football players' shoulders. My mom said she could see him crying all the way from the back of the room.

I keep thinking how did he know all these kids so well? I have never seen someone cheered like that.

After everything settled down, the principal wiggled through the kids back to the mic and asked everyone to sit back down. We did for just a minute and then the program was all over and we threw our caps in the air.

At the very end of everything I went back inside to get my hat. Or anybody's hat. Mom just told me to get one. When I got in there, H.B. was walking down the rows picking up hats and programs. He waved me over and hugged me again.

After all that just happened he said to me, "I'm proud of you, Rex. A lot of kids would have given up." Maybe he said something after that. I don't know. But what he said made me feel proud.

So I told Sparks when I got back out to the parking lot.

And she told me that was a miracle for me.

So here it is in my journal.

Even though he was the real hero today, H.B. told me he was proud of me.

TWENTY-SEVEN

Sparks

MOM CLOSED BOTH THE JOURNAL AND HER EYES.

"I like the rest of the story almost as much as that entry. The reason H.B. hugged Rex was simple: It was for the small miracles Rex performed that spring. None of the kids knew the coach was leaving so when he started acting sad and nostalgic, some of them whispered that he was just getting senile. Rex was different. He recognized the sadness even though he didn't know the source.

"He decided to do or say something nice every time he saw H.B. One day he helped him carry some gear in from the field. Another time he made up a question to ask when they passed in the hall. Even a shared smile and wave brightened both of their days.

"I bet no single encounter lasted more than seventeen seconds but, taken together, they had a huge impact on the man. So what Rex recorded as a kind act by H.B., was also a minor miracle the other direction."

Miles leaned forward. "How do you know the rest of the story? Did you read Sparks's journal?"

"*Read* it? I *wrote* it."

Both boys looked confused.

Kendra and my mother swapped grins.

"Boys, boys, boys," Mom said.

"I know, right?" Kendra said.

The confused looks persisted.

With a sigh and a chuckle, Kendra shared the secret she must have learned in the bathroom. "Mr. Conner's mother *is* Sparks."

TWENTY-EIGHT

Vegas

DAD DIDN'T EVEN UNPACK.

He'd returned from a conference in Las Vegas where he'd represented the station at a trade show. It wasn't long after his transition from accounting to radio.

It was one of Dad's few Seventeen Second Miracles I heard firsthand. Unless I witnessed it, or I heard it later from someone whose life he'd touched, the miracles simply became part of his silent legacy.

Dad gathered Mom and me in the living room and began to talk. "I met the most amazing man this week," he began.

Dad went on to describe the final day of the four-day Vegas convention. Even without his story, I knew that by day four Dad probably knew everyone by first name. And not just those attending the panels or walking the show floor, but the housekeepers, the bellhops, the bellhops' children.

Dad knew no strangers.

One man in particular, a station owner from West Des Moines, Iowa, had become very friendly with Dad.

They met at lunch on the first day and exchanged room numbers and contact information. When Dad told the story, he said he didn't feel right using the man's real name. He called him Bill.

During the convention the two men became fast friends and found they had plenty in common.

Dad was involved with a number of local charities.

Bill was involved with many of the same in West Des Moines.

They both liked to talk politics and history.

They were both married with children.

Dad with one.

Bill with three.

On the final day of the conference, Bill convinced Dad to get up extra early for nine holes of golf, even though they'd probably be late for the morning events. Dad was never an avid golfer, but he enjoyed going out occasionally, particularly if it meant spending time with a friend.

During their round of golf, Bill confided in Dad that he was growing increasingly unhappy with his marriage. *The eleven-and-a-half-year-itch,* he called it. He told Dad that his wife was not the same woman he'd married.

Dad listened.

Admittedly, even when he embarrassed me, even when I convinced myself I hated him, I always appreciated that he listened. Right now, whatever he's doing, I'm convinced he's probably listening now, too.

Dad offered the same kind of advice he'd offered to friends in similar situations: *Stick with it. Don't give up. Be true to her.*

It wasn't groundbreaking marital advice, but Dad delivered it with conviction. He encouraged his new friend to go home and remind himself why he'd married his bride in the first place.

Have you considered that maybe you're not the man she married either?

Bill was thankful for the advice, Dad said, and they completed their round of golf just in time to make the opening gavel of the morning session.

They walked in and sat at the back of the room at a long banquet table with three empty seats. Not long after they settled in for the introductory speaker, a woman in a black skirt and red top snuck in the back door right behind and took the lone remaining seat next to Dad's new friend.

In a half-whisper, the woman shook Bill's hand.

Dad leaned forward and mouthed a *hello* of his own.

Ninety minutes later, the morning emcee announced a fifteen-minute break.

The attendees stood, stretched, rehashed what they'd heard, drank cold coffee in the back of the room, and, according to Dad, began mentally checking out of the long, tiring conference. Despite the fact that the day still had a luncheon, afternoon workshops, and an awards banquet that evening to close the event.

All three stood to enjoy the breather.

Dad formally met the woman with a handshake and his customary routine of get-to-know-you questions that break the ice faster than a meteor. After four or five minutes of friendship building, as Dad called it, he excused himself to the restroom.

He returned as the emcee took his place at the podium, but the seats next to him were empty. He considered looking for Bill and his newest friend, but chose instead to enjoy the discussion onstage.

An hour later he stood, gathered his notes and brochures into his briefcase, and exited the convention center's ballroom. Both his old friend, Bill, the man he'd known all week, and his new friend, the woman he'd met that morning, were sitting in a corner of the lobby chatting.

He thought nothing of it.

The three ate lunch together and attended the first afternoon workshop together.

They separated during the second break because Dad wanted to attend one workshop and Bill and the woman wanted to attend another.

They met again afterward and the woman lamented to both that she hadn't met them earlier in the week.

They sat to chat in one of the hotel lounges.

Dad had water, saying the hot desert air had dried him out.

The man and woman both had whiskey sours.

After drinks, Dad watched for twenty minutes while the others played blackjack.

After blackjack, the three disappeared to their rooms, changed for dinner, and met again in the lobby.

They ate dinner.

The man and woman had glasses of wine.

The woman's laugh became louder. Her *you're-so-funny* arm touches longer. The neckline of her blouse lower.

After the awards were presented and the conference was gaveled to a close, the increasingly flirtatious friends decided to walk the Vegas Strip.

Dad went along.

They visited the Mirage and marveled at the tigers.

Dad stayed close.

They gambled at the MGM and took pictures standing in front of the huge glass windows protecting drunk gamblers from lions and vice versa.

Sometime after 1:00 A.M. they arrived back at Caesars Palace and the couple tried to shed their third wheel.

They sat in three chairs in the lobby near an oversized dollar slot machine.

After a final drink, the woman stood up and whispered something in the man's ear.

He laughed and whispered something back.

Dad said he felt like an idiot when, for the first time all day, he noticed his friend wasn't wearing his wedding ring.

The woman said good night to Dad and offered a wish that they'd bump into each other again sometime. Then she slinked across the lobby and into an elevator.

Bill watched every sway and exaggerated swivel of her hips. When he turned his attention back to my father, he saw that Dad had slid his chair as close as he could get it.

Dad held three wallet-sized pictures in his hand. A family

portrait. A picture of Mom smiling from a lawn chair, and my ninth-grade class picture.

He explained some history behind each photo and counted the number of times the man looked toward the elevator or grabbed a glance at his watch.

When he was through, he asked his friend if he had any pictures to share in return.

The man did, and Dad quizzed him about each.

When was this taken?

What position does he play?

She's tall, how old did you say she was again?

She has your wife's eyes.

Two hours later, the man gave my father a hug and said he was going to his room to call home, despite the late hour, and sleep.

Dad didn't doubt for a second.

The next morning they'd planned to meet to share a cab to the airport. But when Dad checked out of the hotel, there was a note from the man waiting for him at the front desk. It read: *Changed my flight and am flying home as soon as possible. Thank you. For everything. You may have saved me from drowning my marriage.*

We called this Dad's one and only Seventeen *Hour* Miracle.

TWENTY-NINE

Rope

THEY PASSED IN A BLUR.

The days leading to our next Discussion were unusually overscheduled for me, particularly for November. The firm suddenly needed my attention every day. One of my wealthiest clients, Marci Wright, a multimillionaire with assets and holdings around the world, had received a letter from the IRS advising that she was being audited. She was justifiably unhappy, but her grandson was livid.

Jade's lease at Paper Gems was up for renewal and the landlord was making the negotiation for a new deal much more difficult than it needed to be. He didn't care that independent bookstores were struggling or that the building needed a new heating and air-conditioning system.

Then, out of nowhere, two prominent members of the local chamber of commerce had approached me about running for Charlottesville City Council. I wasn't interested, but they read my disinterest as a desire to be arm-twisted. They came to my home twice to make their case, and twice I sat on the porch with them and politely declined.

For the first time since they started, the Discussions and my three students were on my mind much less than the reality of my own life.

For the first time, I wasn't counting the minutes until Friday at 5:30.

It was a struggle I'd fought before. The young men and women who'd graced my life had a unique talent for becoming important to me. They listened. They absorbed the history.

It became all too easy to become lost in my own life, my own lessons, and in Dad's legacy. Sometimes I don't think of the future often enough.

One summer night seven years ago, I walked in the front door for dinner. I'd had a difficult Discussion with my group that morning and shared my frustrations with Jade during an afternoon phone call from my office to the back room of Paper Gems. Back then, as I exhaled at the end of that long day, I found a twelve-inch piece of fat braided rope on my plate. She had hand-painted each of the three braids a different color: red, yellow, and blue.

"Uh, honey, everything OK?" I asked.

"Sit," she said, and she sat across from me.

With the rope in my hands, Jade explained that the red braid was my life, the yellow braid my father's, and the blue was my students'. "This rope is your summer, Cole. You bring these kids to the porch and you braid together the lessons of his life, your life, and their lives."

"OK, I follow, I suppose."

"Notice anything about the rope?" she asked.

"It's short?"

"What else?"

"It's on my plate when I was expecting pasta?" I teased.

She came and knelt behind me, taking the rope from my hands. "Look closer." She spun the rope in a circle, the colors spinning like a barbershop pole.

"There are three braids. Each is painted. And they all touch each other?"

"That's right. And each is equal in size, right?"

"Indeed they are."

Jade coaxed my knees out from underneath the table and eased toward me, putting her hands on my cheeks. "Sweetheart, always remember these Discussions of yours, this program, it isn't just about your dad, and it's certainly not just about you. It's about the kids, too, and what they stand to learn. It's about *their* lives."

I wondered how long she'd wanted to have this conversation.

"It's about the past, the present, and future, right?"

"Of course."

"So, Cole, ask yourself this: What's the point of all these lessons, the stories of your father, the memory of Flick, if they don't point to the future?"

THIRTY

Field Trip

IT WAS THE FIRST TIME TRAVIS HAD ARRIVED FIRST.

I met him as he got out of the van and took the chance to say hello to his mother. She said good-bye to Travis and retracted the wheelchair ramp into the van.

When Travis didn't immediately wheel himself down the walk and toward the store, she invited him to.

"Travis, I'd like to speak to Mr. Conner, please." She continued only when he'd made it out of earshot.

"What can I do for you, Mrs. Nielson? I'm sorry—*Beth*."

She looked left and right, presumably for the other students. "May I be blunt?"

"Of course," I said, though I was actually thinking, *Uh-oh.*

"Are you making progress with Travis?"

I couldn't decide if it was a trick question or not. "I'm afraid that's not an easy answer, Beth."

"Why?"

"Because every student is different. And quite honestly, I don't even know what defines *progress* yet. But I can assure you he's having a good experience."

She fumbled with her keychain.

"Sometimes he comes home in a good mood, sometimes he's angry about something." She looked around again for other curious ears. "I've lost my job. And it's a long drive, Mr. Conner. It's a long drive over here and gas is expensive. And when I ask Travis what you talk about, what your *Discussions* are about, he says he doesn't really know. I just want to know if it's helping him."

I put my hand on her arm. "I can't tell you to what degree it's helping. But I can tell you I've been at this for over a decade, and the lessons the kids take away can change them."

Her crossed arms and defensive stance screamed, *Does he need changing?*

"We're having a good time, and if he keeps asking you to bring him, then it's probably worthwhile. That's my opinion."

She glanced at the store, then back to me. "Has he told you what happened?"

"With?"

"With his legs. The reason he's in the wheelchair."

I shook my head.

"When he trusts you, he will. It's our arrangement. I'm not allowed to talk about it with anyone but him. It's his story to tell when he's ready."

"I understand."

"No, you don't. Not yet. When he tells you, you'll understand why he didn't want to come back after you told the story about the boy who let the little girl drown."

The description stung, but I was still pleased that Travis had shared the story of Flick with his mother.

Laughter startled us from the corner where alley met mall. Between a tree growing unnaturally out of the brick pedestrian mall and a much more at-home lamppost, we saw Jade standing by Travis. It appeared she was reading from a book.

Travis laughed again.

I looked back at his mother, but she was already rounding the front of the van.

I saw a smile, though a guarded one, as she got in the van.

Just as Travis's mother pulled out of her customary parking place, Kendra and Miles pulled into the one before it. We all joined Jade and Travis on the mall.

"What's so funny up here?" I asked.

Jade held up a book she'd been reading that week and grinned at Travis. "You had to be there," she said.

"You want to stick around for a field trip?" I asked her.

But before she could answer, Kendra said, "We're going on a field trip? Cool."

"Just down to the end of the mall and back."

"Cool," she repeated.

The confusion on Jade's face was both obvious and rare. "What field trip?"

"You'll see."

Jade threw her hands up. "Why not? Store is covered this evening. Don't need to be there until closing. I'm in."

I asked everyone to line up, turn, and face the store.

"What do you see?" I asked.

"My store," Jade snarked.

"Nice try, new kid." I walked down the line and stood behind Miles. "How about you. What do you see?"

"The bookstore? Paper Gems?"

"Better." I slapped him on the back.

"Kendra, what do *you* see?"

"A classroom?" she answered.

"Even better." I reached between her and Miles with my fist. She tapped my knuckles with hers.

I moved to the end of the line and stood directly behind Travis's wheelchair. I put my hands on his shoulders. "Travis, hearing what they've said, what do you see when you look up there?"

I felt his shoulders shrug beneath my hands.

"We know it's a store and a classroom. What can you add to those descriptions?"

He looked from the store to me. "A warm place?"

It was not what I was looking for, but it felt right anyway. "Anything else?"

He took his cap off, this one bearing the Cleveland Cavaliers logo, and rubbed the top of his head. "Not really."

"Very good." I stepped out in front of them. "Think of that store behind me as a classroom. That is where we've learned the origin of the Seventeen Second Miracles. We know how valuable it is to perform at least one each day; we've seen it in theory and history." I pointed with my thumb over my right shoulder. "Now, turn around and face the street."

As they did, Jade slowed long enough to mouth the words, *Oh, THAT field trip.*

"If the store is the classroom for the Seventeen Second Miracle," I continued, "then the mall, the city, the world, they are the lab." I stepped to the curb. "Follow me. We're going to see some Seventeen Second Miracles in action."

Like little ducklings, we started down the brick-paved "street." I led the way, and Kendra, Miles, Travis, and Jade followed in a line. We proceeded toward the heart of Charlottesville's historic shopping area. After a block, I turned and spoke as I walked backward. "I want you to pay attention to what's happening around you. If you see someone performing a miracle for someone, stop us. If you see anything at all that might qualify as a Seventeen Second Miracle, shout it out."

"This is really exciting," Kendra said and took Miles's hand in hers.

"Yeah, it's different," he answered as they walked along.

I drifted to the back of our little procession. Travis was rolling down the center of the sidewalk; Jade, his new friend, walked at his side.

As I had many times already that November, I thought, *I wish my father were here.*

"Oh, I almost forgot, everyone got your pocket watches?"

Kendra pulled hers and Miles's from her purse.

Travis slapped his front pocket.

I gave him a thumbs-up and went back to the front of the line.

At the end of the second block we slowed near an art gallery whose front door was being held partway open. As we passed by I waved and said hello to an older gentleman standing with his foot in the door.

"I'm ready when you are, Donna," the man said to someone unseen through the open door.

A moment later, a woman appeared and I motioned for the group to slow down. I motioned toward the couple. The man held the door open with his back as he took the woman's arm and gently guided her down two stone steps.

After she was safe and steady, he held his arm out for her and she took firm hold of it. They moved along in perfect lock step.

Once the couple was a block away, I asked, "Anyone see that?"

"I did," Kendra said.

"And?"

"It was sweet. Right, Mrs. Conner?"

"It was," Jade answered.

"Was it a Seventeen Second Miracle?" I asked.

Travis rolled his chair closer. "He just opened the door for his lady."

"And?"

"That's it."

"You don't think that was an act of service? A little miracle for her?"

Travis looked at the others for backup. "He's probably done it, like, a billion times."

"And?"

Kendra stepped back into the conversation. "It's a habit for him now. We learned that in psychology. He probably doesn't even think about it anymore. He probably just does it. That's what makes it so sweet to me."

Miles's hands were in his pockets. "I open doors for you."

"Sometimes," Kendra said, without looking over her shoulder.

"Let's walk," I said.

We spotted two coeds on the opposite side of the street in conversation. One was wearing jogging clothes and a knit cap; the other had a backpack on her shoulder.

"See them?" I pointed casually without drawing too much attention. "Don't stare, but do you see the girls across the mall there?"

Nods and *uh-huhs* from the group.

"What do you think they're talking about?"

Miles answered first. "Who knows? Whatever girls talk about. Clothes, dudes, makeup. Right, Travis?"

"Yup." He flashed two sideways peace signs.

Kendra looked at Jade and displayed a dramatic eye-roll.

"What's your opinion, Jade?"

She stepped around Travis and split Miles and Kendra.

"I'll tell you exactly."

I knew what came next. It was precisely why I asked.

"Hi, Bev." Jade watched the women intently.

"Hi, Bonnie." Both voices were Jade's. Two-way imagined conversations were a Jade Conner specialty.

"How are you?"

"Groovy. How are you?"

The kids began to laugh at Jade's one-woman show.

"I heard about you and Digbert McCrackin Face. I'm sorry. You were such a cute couple."

"It's OK, he wasn't right for me anyway."

"That's right, girl, you deserve so much better than that guy. He's not Prince Charming."

I heard Miles whisper to Travis, "Dude, I can't tell which voice is which."

Jade continued, "Let's get together sometime. Maybe a mani-pedi? Frozen yogurt?" Her hands were flying through the air like a pizza chef.

"Great! I'd love that. That would get my mind off him for sure. And maybe we could get tats after."

It was my turn to join the laughter. Jade and I enjoyed this game sometimes when we could get away with it without being caught or embarrassing anyone. It had been an entertaining diversion many times while sitting in gridlocked traffic headed north out of town on 29.

As I began to subtly applaud, the strangers across the street hugged and continued in their opposite directions. One jogging, one walking with a broad smile on her face.

The kids joined in the applause and Jade took a deep bow.

"What just happened?" I asked when the giggles subsided.

"Your wife lost her wattage?" Travis said.

"Besides that. Miles, take a stab here."

He looked at Jade and held his hands out for help.

She pointed at him confidently.

"Mrs. Conner pretended to talk like them. Like she was both ladies."

"And?"

"She was pretty funny."

"True dat," Travis piped in.

"And?" I continued looking at Miles.

"Maybe that's what they were really talking about. Not the exact words. But maybe one of them has been sad or whatever. And they bumped into each other."

"Outstanding, Miles."

"Kendra?"

"I think they were headed in different directions. The one jogging stopped the other one to say hello. Maybe Miles and Mrs. Conner are right. Maybe the other one is sad about something. So it was like a nice random meeting."

"Maybe the meeting was random, the passing on the street at this exact time, but the decision to stop and chat, to be friendly, that wasn't random, was it?"

"But that doesn't happen to everyone, Mr. C."

"It doesn't, Travis?"

"Not to me."

I waved him closer with both hands. "Explain."

"People don't always do that junk, that's all. People don't stop me like that and ask whatever."

"Never?"

"Not really." He took his hat off and rubbed his head.

That was the moment our time together changed.

Why hadn't I taken just a minute—just one single minute—to ask Jade her opinion?

To reflect?

To breathe?

To think, *What would Dad do?*

Our field trip might have ended much differently.

THIRTY-ONE

Experiment

"FOLLOW ME."

The group fell behind in procession as we continued past the center courtyard of the mall and toward another row of businesses. The fall sun continued sinking in the sky, its warmth overcome by the evening chill. At least the wind wasn't blowing.

Travis and Miles were directly behind me.

Miles was in track pants and a basketball jersey under his letterman's jacket.

Travis wore baggy carpenter overalls, Crocs, and a Washington Redskins sweatshirt.

Jade and Kendra lagged farther behind, walking side by side and visiting.

Jade was in a lime-green skirt and top under a long black jacket.

Kendra wore pink sweatpants and, most odd, given the cool weather, a light blue polo.

We approached a drugstore that had probably been there when the downtown mall was a street used by horse-drawn carriages.

I gathered them around me, off to the side of the entrance.

"Ready for an experiment?"

They each nodded an uncertain *yes*, but Jade looked concerned.

"Travis, you're going to be my guinea pig. That all right?"

"I guess."

I stepped closer to him and dug my wallet from my back pocket. "I'm going to give you twenty dollars and send you inside. I want you to buy a bag of snacks. Chips, candy bars, whatever. Something we can all eat on the way back."

"Uh, all right." He took the money from me. "Can I keep the change?"

"We'll see." I laughed. "When you come out, I want you to have the bag on your lap, all right?"

"But I usually hook that kinda stuff on my chair."

"I understand, Travis. Just this time, for me, put it on your lap."

"Weird, but whatever," he conceded.

"Jade, Miles, and Kendra are going to walk away and watch. I'm going to pretend like I don't know you when you come out, and we'll bump into each other. Then we're going to give people an opportunity to serve. I think you'll be amazed at what you see."

"I don't know, Mr. Conner."

"Trust me, Travis."

Travis posed a couple of nervous questions and rolled his way into the store. A customer leaving held the door for him and Travis mumbled a thank-you.

Jade sidled up next to me. "Do you know what you're doing, sweetheart?"

"I think so," I said, and hoped I was right.

No, I *prayed* I was I right.

Jade's countenance said she was worried, and I was grateful she trusted me enough not to press.

"You two still have those pocket watches?"

Miles and Kendra both answered yes, and Kendra again retrieved them from her purse.

"Watch those," I said, "and let's see how long it takes a miracle to happen."

Jade gave my arm a gentle, encouraging squeeze, and led Miles and Kendra to a bench two storefronts away.

I retreated a few yards and waited.

As I stood nervously watching the store's glass double doors, I wondered whether my dad would have approved of my field experiment. He'd been the one to teach me that discussing the joy of service and the legacy of the Seventeen Second Miracle was wonderful, but that putting it into action was what made it all matter.

"History is a blessing," he had said. "But only because it teaches us to live better."

His words had been proven true many times in my life and in my Discussions. But now, as I waited for Travis to emerge, my nerves jumped and the doubts began to gather energy.

Before I could harness that energy into a second thought,

Travis emerged from the store with a white plastic sack of snack food sitting precariously on his knees.

He rolled five feet out, looking anxiously right, then left.

Then a few feet more.

I put my cell phone to my right ear and pretended to talk.

Then I jumped from my position and walked by him, giving the illusion of being lost in concentration.

I bumped his chair hard with my legs, and with my left hand helped slide the bag violently off his knees. The momentum sent the bag flying before him to the ground. Half of the items spilled onto the sidewalk.

A box of Tic-Tacs.

A bag of Route 11 potato chips.

A Heath Bar.

A Moon Pie.

A bottle of Grape Fanta rolled down the sidewalk.

A roll of Rolos did the same.

"Sorry, pal," I said and I walked briskly on. Ten seconds later, I passed Kendra, Miles, and Jade on the bench.

Miles was studying the face of his pocket watch looking stunned.

Kendra's hands covered her mouth; her eyes were wide.

Jade had stood and I discreetly shook my head when we briefly made eye contact.

At the end of the block, I pretended to dial a new number and turned around.

Travis looked like he'd been hit by a truck.

The Fanta had come to a stop against a *Daily Progress* newspaper box.

A young coed carrying a gym bag walked by with headphones in her ears and a bounce in her step.

Two young men, each on longboards, skated past.

Travis's eyes were fixed on the sidewalk.

Jade turned to find me, her hands extended, pleading to help.

I held up a finger and whispered, "Just wait, please," even though she couldn't have possibly heard me.

I looked at my own watch.

Ten seconds.

Twenty seconds.

It had been at least thirty since I'd knocked into him.

Could I have been this wrong?

I could tell Travis's eye line had moved from the sidewalk to his lap. His head was down and his chin nearly touched his chest.

My heart sank as a woman in a hospital lab coat walked by, utterly oblivious.

Then another.

Then someone on a bike.

A couple holding hands.

Looking back on those moments, I cannot say with any certainty how many seconds had passed. What I do know is that it felt like minutes, even hours, before Miles finally jumped off the bench and jogged toward Travis.

He bent over and retrieved the Rolos, the Fanta, the Tic-Tacs, the chips, and set them on Travis's lap.

I began to walk back to the scene. Slowly, shyly, looking everywhere but at Jade.

I was the last to arrive.

I was the last to realize Travis was crying.

We walked like an unhappy army of ants back to Paper Gems, and the return trip felt twice as far.

Kendra and Jade strolled up front on either side of Travis's wheelchair, dodging fire hydrants and other pedestrians.

Miles and I walked at least twenty yards behind.

Travis's familiar van was waiting in the alley when we arrived. Mrs. Nielson began waving from the corner when she saw us.

Jade and I waved back.

Travis moved away from the group and rolled right past his mother. He stopped at the door of the van.

"Hi, Travis," Mrs. Nielson said. "Have fun?"

"Can we go?" he said.

I took a step closer. "Could I have one more minute with him, Beth?"

"Of course," she answered, and Jade took her by the hand to show her the details of her Babes in Toyland window display.

"I'm sorry, Travis." I got on one knee at his side.

His eyes were locked on the van.

"I expected something different, Travis. I promise you I did not mean for you to be embarrassed."

Without looking up, Travis reached into his pocket and forcefully pulled the pocket watch from his front pocket. Holding it by the chain, he flung it far onto the pavement. It slid nearly ten feet.

"Can we talk about it?"

No reply.

"Next week?"

Stillness.

"I'm sorry, Travis. I cannot say it enough."

I'd known embarrassment.

I'd known pain.

But the regret I felt, the deepness of the remorse, was so foreign to me I didn't know whether to cry or shout.

So I did neither. I just stood up and backed away.

Miles surprised me when he knelt beside Travis. He whispered something. He twisted his hat around on his head so the bill faced backward. Then he held up a fist and didn't put it down until a very reluctant Travis "pounded" it.

"That's amazing, Mrs. Conner . . . Sorry, Jade," Travis's mother said, returning to the van. "Thank you." She opened the van door and lowered the lift.

Kendra, Miles, and Jade all shouted *good-byes* and *See ya laters* as Travis disappeared into the darkness of the van.

His mother smiled a quiet good-bye and drove off.

I couldn't even wave as she pulled away.

I retrieved Travis's watch. It worked, but it was badly beaten.

THIRTY-TWO

Rex's Journal

December 23, 1998

I never tire of the miracles!

Today's show was exceptional, I think. I interviewed the Swinsons, a young couple from the Staunton area who have the most inspirational story I've brought to the show in a long time.

This struggling young couple received an anonymous gift last month in the mail. A cashier's check for $10,000 from someone who said they'd touched his life. They don't know who it might have been. Not a clue.

They were so touched by someone's generosity that they decided to pass it on. They said they donated $1,000 to their church, then they asked the bank for ninety $100 bills. They put them in individual envelopes and handed them out to people they thought might appreciate it in the parking lots at Wal-Mart and 7-Eleven.

They gave away $9,000 in cash!

This is money they could have saved, lived off of, used to pay for diapers and formula for their baby. Instead they gave it away and spread the joy.

Someone heard about their generosity from a friend at the bank. The bank called the paper. The paper ran a story. The station manager at WCHV saw the story and called me.

But when I spoke to them on the phone they were adamant about not going on the air. The sweet wife kept saying they hadn't done it for attention. But when I explained the concept of the Seventeen Second Miracle and how I'd used the show to promote the concept of daily giving, the woman softened.

When I offered to change their names when they came on air, they both agreed.

Today was the interview, and it was miraculous! Their story and the pureness really moved me. The phones lit up with people wanting to thank them for their example. Of course a few crackpots called in to call them idiots and admit they would have bought a new television or taken a trip with the money, but the overwhelming majority supported their decision.

But the miracle that belongs in the journal happened afterward. As I was leaving the station for the day, the receptionist, Rosie, stopped me at the elevator. She said, "Rex, thank you for bringing them on the show." Rosie actually had tears in her eyes!

I gave her a big hug and told her she was welcome.

She said thank you one more time and walked away.

Rosie thanked me today and made all the work for today's interview worth it.

THIRTY-THREE

Coach

I SPENT THE EVENING OF THE EXPERIMENT ON MY PORCH.

Jade and I read from one of my father's journals. Some entries made us laugh; some made us think.

Jade stayed as long as she could before leaving to close Paper Gems.

When she left, my instincts told me to get in my car and drive to Travis's house and camp in his front yard until he agreed to see me.

I wanted to apologize—again—and to explain myself.

But I wasn't sure there was much of an explanation to offer.

The world had failed me the one time I most needed it not to.

Mom and I both remember that Dad had his share of disappointments, and we'd reminisced about them before. The times Dad held open a door for a woman who bypassed him and opened another. Or who passed through but didn't make eye contact or offer even a muted *Thank you.*

Once, Dad stopped to help a woman change a tire in the parking lot of a church on Cherry Avenue. Dad said the woman reached back into the car when she saw him approaching and pulled out a can of Mace big enough to wipe out every sex offender and tire-changer between Richmond and Waynesboro.

He apologized for bothering her and continued approaching until she unleashed a tirade of profanity about not getting fooled again. Dad said he was sorry and drove off.

I reached down to the wooden floor of the porch and picked up a cup of hot chocolate. It was more chocolate than hot, and I stepped into the house, surrendering the porch to the cold night.

When I returned to the porch to retrieve the journals, a tall, broad man with a Val Kilmer–like *Top Gun* haircut was waiting for me.

"Mr. Conner?"

"Yes, may I help you?" I extended my hand and he gave it a firm, confident, perhaps compensating shake.

"I'm Coach Max, Kendra's father."

Of course, I thought, *the resemblance is striking.* "Very nice to meet you, Max."

"Call me Coach."

I couldn't be sure whether it was a polite offer made in hoped-for friendship, or an order. Given his enormous arms and bulging neck, I decided it didn't matter.

"Perfect. Good to make your acquaintance, *Coach*. Would you like to come in?"

"Can you tell me what these classes of yours are all about?" He apparently did not want to come in.

I offered him a seat.

He declined.

I offered him a hot chocolate.

He declined that, too.

"The Discussions are about seeing the world differently. They're about thinking beyond ourselves and about learning the habit of daily kindness."

"This was Buhl's idea?"

"What exactly?"

"The class."

"Not exactly, no. But he's been a partner for many years. His father was among my father's best friends and knew all about Dad's Seventeen Second Miracles. Now his son is in a position to support the concept." I breathed. "Principal Buhl is a good man."

"Uh-huh." Coach Max appeared to be studying the porch.

"Is there a problem, Coach? Something specific you want to talk about?" I noticed that his head was nearly level with the top of the porch swing. I calculated how tall that made him. *6' 4"?*

"Listen, I'm sure your little chat time helps some kids. But right now, frankly, they're a distraction."

"To Kendra?"

"Miles," he corrected. "He's off, and I think your bull sessions are the reason."

I was trying to decide what to do with my arms and hands in the shadow of this intimidating figure. *Fold them? Hands in pocket? Hands on hips?*

I went for the pocket look. "I understand your concerns,

Coach. And I'm very grateful you shared them. I know we've had a few challenging days and I've pushed the kids. But I think the experience will be good for Miles if he—"

"Wait," he said and put his hand up in the air. His palm must have been two feet wide. I could barely see his chest. "What if Miles stops coming?"

"Well—"

"Let me finish. What happens if he doesn't finish? Does he not graduate next spring?"

"Of course not," I said.

"Affect a scholarship to play ball somewhere?"

"Probably not."

He pressed on each of his temples with his fat thumbs.

"Coach, I think he ought to be the one to decide, or at least in consultation with his parents, don't you?" The boldness impressed me. *I wish Jade were here,* I thought.

"During basketball season, I *am* his parents. And that time is now." His giant wing was up before my mouth was open for a rebuttal. "He's done. That kid is a force on the basketball court and he has a chance to play in college. Maybe not the ACC or the Southeastern Conference, but somewhere with a free ride. If Kendra wants to keep coming to the sessions, that's her play to call." He shook my hand again, even more firmly than the last time, and my most of my knuckles cracked.

"I think you're making a mistake, Mr. Wilson."

He turned and walked down the steps. Without the courtesy of looking back, he said, "Maybe, but don't you make a bigger one."

THIRTY-FOUR

Forgiveness

It was one of the last times I truly embarrassed my father.

I knew because he told me.

As a freshman in high school, I had been fortunate enough to make the right kinds of friends. Or at least the right kinds of friends in the eyes of an attention-craving fourteen-year-old.

Much to my surprise, I made the freshman basketball team. I wasn't very good, but neither were any of the other incoming freshmen that year. In fact, by comparison, I was arguably one of the stars of the team. What I lacked in coordination I made up for in size with my broad shoulders and quick feet. I didn't handle the ball well, but I got up and down the court quicker than most and could grab any missed shot that came even close to my *zip code*, as the coach called it.

Being on the basketball team, even with our losing record that fall of my freshmen year, opened my world of friends beyond anything I could have predicted on the first day of school. Most of the members of the JV team—comprised primarily of sopho-mores and juniors—talked to me at lunch and gave me high fives when I passed in between classes.

Even some of the varsity team members knew my name and would nod or otherwise acknowledge me.

This familiarity, though still shallow, also introduced me into another important social world: cheerleaders. I remember running down the court during our first home game with a wide-open layup and hearing the cheerleaders shout my name: "Go, Cole! Make that shot! Goooooo!"

Who needs alcohol? I thought. *Can you get any more drunk than I feel right now?*

By the end of my freshmen year, I might have been the most popular ninth grader in school. I wasn't the smartest, I wasn't the best looking, and I certainly wasn't the most athletic, but I was very good at putting myself in the right places at the right time to meet the right people and say the right things. I was a member of more cliques than the entire basketball team—*combined*.

At that point in our family, Dad was settling into his second career in the radio business and Mother was still working in human resources at the university. Dad's miracles were a part of our lives every single day, and at dinner we often went around the table and reported back on the small and simple things we'd done for one another, or the things that had been done to us. Dad's rule, and it was one Mom supported, was that we not brag about what we'd done for someone. But, we could take credit if asked.

This chatter at home about charity and service didn't bother me because I'd been on the receiving end more times than any journal could possibly hold.

Sometimes my father's daily Seventeen Second Miracles were harmless to me. Flowers for someone at work. Loaning someone a couple bucks at lunch. Offering to babysit someone's kids on the weekend when I was gone with friends anyway.

Other times his miracles were so embarrassing I walked away, pretended not to know him, rebelled later with words and action I now regret.

One such experience changed the nature of our relationship forever.

With two weeks to go in the school year and finals wrapped up for the semester, some of the guys on the freshmen team had gotten permission to shoot around in the gym after school. The pretense was getting a head start on the next year and the junior varsity tryouts, which would happen before school actually started in the fall. The truth was most of us just wanted to hang out together. We knew despite our best efforts to *stay cool* and *keep in touch* during the summer, as we'd promised in one another's yearbooks, summer vacations and busy parents would prevent consistent opportunities to hang out.

One afternoon we met in the gym after the final bell and played until the janitors kicked us out at 5:30. Most of us went outside to the school's main entrance and gathered by the flag-pole to wait for our rides.

Also waiting outside, presumably for their ride, were two foreign exchange students from Japan. They were brothers, we thought, because they looked alike. But none of us had classes with them and we only knew that they spoke tattered English because we'd heard older kids tease them.

Three of the guys hanging out with my group, Matthew, Eric, and Funk, started mocking the Japanese students. Matthew pulled his eyelids tight and said, "Ching chong choo, egg rolls and rice."

The exchange students glanced over, but just as quickly averted their eyes back to the ground.

Eric and Funk took their turns and cut the distance between our group and them in half. They put their hands together and bowed. "Kung Foo Chicken," one of them yelled. "I am Karate Kid!"

"Wax on, wax off," said the other, crouching down and wiping his hands across the air in big circles.

Matthew became more bold and shouted, "You work Panda Express? You make noodles? You give free chopsticks?"

Funk and Eric laughed.

So I did, too, as each barb and jab cut deeper.

Then Dad pulled up.

I gave a cool *Later* to the guys and gathered up my backpack. I wish I'd been more prepared to jump in Dad's car.

I also wish the boys had stopped their teasing sooner.

Before I could get to the passenger's door, Dad had already turned off the engine and hopped out.

"What's up, champs?" Dad said.

If I'd rolled my eyes any further, they would have popped out of my head and rolled across the parking lot.

"Hi, Mr. Conner," Funk said through laughter.

Dad looked at the foreign exchange students. "Who are your friends?"

Funk, Eric, and Matthew looked at one another nervously. "Just some kids," Eric said and then looked at me. "They work at Panda Express," he said in a whisper-chortle.

I wish I'd been close enough to slap him in the back of the head.

Dad looked at the students again. "You ever met them?"

Panicky head shakes for four, please.

"Let's go." He spun away and began walking toward them. When he realized we weren't behind him, he looked at us and said, "Or I can bring them over here."

"Dad, stop. They're just foreign exchange students. They'll be gone soon anyway."

But he kept walking.

"Dad, you're going to embarrass me. Stop. *Please.*"

Dad arrived at the two timid Japanese exchange students and began talking. I was too far to hear what he'd said, but after just a few seconds he shook their hands and waved us over.

Matthew, Funk, and Eric all went and shook their hands, too.

I watched as the Japanese students gave subtle, instinctive bows of thanks.

It appeared Dad excused himself and said good-bye. My friends stayed standing in a circle with the Japanese boys. One of them said something funny and they all laughed, even though I was sure the Japanese boys didn't understand a word.

Dad got into the car and I followed, slipping into the passenger's seat and seething.

Dad didn't say a word.

I said three: *I hate you.*

Not long after dinner that night, eaten in relative quiet, Dad knocked on my door and invited himself in. He found me reading *MAD Magazine.*

"Homework done?" He sat on the edge of my bed.

"Uh-huh."

"Good work. Anything you need help with?"

I shook my head and turned the page.

"Listen to me, Cole. About today: I'm sorry I put you on the spot in front of your friends."

I turned another page.

Dad seemed to think for a bit before making more futile attempts to strike up a casual, meaningless conversation and I ignored him, offering only intermittent grunts and *Uh-huhs.*

After a prolonged and, I was convinced, well-planned period of silence between us, Dad said, "You know what, Son, we're a lot alike." He stood up and opened my door. "The only difference is that I'd already forgiven you before even coming in the room."

THIRTY-FIVE

Rekindling Flames

Two nights later, Jade surprised me.

We drove to Washington, D.C., for an opera at the Kennedy Center and a late dinner in Chinatown. Jade looked a vision in her long black dress and heels, and the show was entertaining. But dinner was even better. We savored Peking duck with scrumptious slices of duck, Mandarin pancakes, and hoisin sauce.

We talked about everything but Kendra, Miles, Travis, and Coach Max Wilson.

We talked about Mom and her string of good luck: four properties sold in one month in a terrible market.

We talked about the Christmas sale at Paper Gems and the latest Kevin Milne novel.

We dreamt about the coming summer and our promised plans for an extended vacation. We debated the options.

Jade suggested renting a home for a month in France.

I suggested backpacking all throughout Europe, camping and

staying in hostels. We'd travel country by country via high-speed train.

Jade exercised one of her vacation vetoes.

We discussed South America, a beach house in Mexico, an Alaskan cruise, an African safari, walking atop the Great Wall of China.

After dinner, Jade opened her fortune cookie while I signed the credit card slip. We added *at the zoo* to the end of each fortune, a longtime family custom.

"Your immediate future is white hot—at the zoo," she read.

I opened mine. *"Always enjoy the long way home—at the zoo."*

We tossed them on the table and wound our way to the Metro stop.

The Orange line sent us under the Potomac River into Virginia. We sped through Rosslyn and trendy Ballston to our car parked in the back of the brightly lit parking garage in West Falls Church.

I drove halfway home. We stopped in Culpeper for gas, caffeine, and two ice cream sandwiches.

Jade drove the rest of the forty-five miles home to Charlottesville and we sang almost every Coldplay and Rascal Flatts song we knew.

At 2:00 A.M., Jade's phone rang. We looked at each other and hoped it was a pocket-dial or wrong number. There is no such thing as good news at that time of night.

"This is Jade. Uh-huh. What's wrong, Candace? Just tell me. No. Oh no. We'll be there as soon as we can."

"What is it, sweetheart?"

"There's been a fire."

At 2:30 a.m., we entered the northern edges of Charlottesville driving at what my mother would call "throw you under the jail" speeds. The streets were quiet, especially for a Friday. We cut across Rio Road and into downtown.

As we turned onto Main Street, a wide avenue but with only one lane in each direction, a Charlottesville police cruiser raced up behind us, its lights flashing and siren singing.

It followed us into the alley.

"You can't park here," the cop said through Jade's open window. Before she could say anything, he added, "Turn around in that spot and find somewhere else to park." I nodded to indicate we would just waste more time arguing with him.

Jade turned around and parked on the street a block away.

We walked down the next side street, passing a large fire truck and a fire chief's white-and-orange sedan. Then we turned the corner.

I stopped breathing while I processed the image, because there are sights no human being deserves to see, no matter how they've chosen to live their life.

There were more fire trucks, an ambulance, police cars, and a Red Cross van parked in front of Paper Gems. *Jade's Paper Gems.*

Smoke poured into the air through the shattered front windows and transformed the pulsating yellow, red, blue, and white lights into a grey mess.

A massive firefighter stopped us both, one with each arm. "Too close, too close," he yelled.

Jade dropped to her knees.

If I could have spoken, I think I would have said:

But that's her store. And it might as well be her home. Do you know that? Do you know the books on the shelves are part of my wife's soul? Books Jade has had a week. Books she's had since the shop opened. The very book she was reading the day we first met in the sand at Virginia Beach is in her office here. There are dozens of children's books she's had since her mother used to read them to her at bedtime. Children's books she hoped to read to our own children someday. Books she hoped to put in the little hands of other people's children. That's her store.

THIRTY-SIX

Ash

JADE AND I SPENT THE REST OF THE NIGHT WATCHING.

We watched the firefighters as they poked through ashes looking for hidden flames. Framed by the glassless window openings, they were a tragic window display. *Now available at Paper Gems: Burnt Dreams.*

We watched police come and go. More than we'd ever needed.

Red Cross volunteers come and go. More than we'd ever needed.

The return of Candace, Jade's right hand at Paper Gems. She'd run home to check on her kids and wouldn't stop apologizing for it. She used her floppy arms to pull Jade into her ample bosom.

We watched the sun come up, like a curtain at the opera, to reveal what had happened onstage.

All we could see through the windows was blackness.

The fire captain stood with us just inside the yellow tape.

"The news is good, Mr. and Mrs. Conner. It looks worse than it is, believe me."

I was certain Jade would have punched him if she weren't too tired to make a fist.

"Our guys will know more now that the sun's up, but it sure looks like the fire started up front. Most of the damage to the store is in the display area. We got on scene extremely quickly."

When we didn't reply right way, he added, "You're lucky. Those window displays went up like kindling. Another ten minutes and we would be looking at an empty shell."

I put my arm around Jade and pulled her in.

She stood at my side, shivering, still wearing her dress and light jacket from the night before.

"When can we get inside?" I asked.

He looked over at the store. "I'm betting we'll clear it in another couple hours. Depends on what the guys say, obviously."

"How long before we'll know what started it?"

"Officially? A few days. A week. Hard to say." He took his hat off and set it on the sidewalk. "Unofficially?"

"Sure."

"This was arson."

Jade's eyes shot open and her hands flew to her mouth.

"That can't be," I said.

He put one of his callused hands on my shoulder. "I could be wrong. But I've been to a lot of fires, bud. This has the look of it."

Tears began to drip through a patch of ash on Jade's cheek.

I looked back at him. "Thank you for everything."

"Of course," he answered. "And like I said, I could be wrong."

He offered condolences and then went back to work. Hoses were retracted onto the two main trucks, statements recorded, neighbors questioned, department pictures taken. By 8:00 A.M., a photographer from the paper was taking pictures for the next day's paper.

The Red Cross had stayed throughout the dawn hours providing enough coffee, blankets, and snacks for ten fires. At every break in the action they hugged us and asked what more they could do.

My mother arrived with boxes of donuts, granola bars and bottles of juice, and a big thermos of coffee. She held Jade and repeated over and over, "I'm so glad you weren't here working late."

Investigators arrived at 9:00 and took even more photos. They interviewed neighbors, canvassed three or four blocks in every direction, and quizzed us about old lamps and new furnaces. *How old was the wiring? Were there candles in the displays? Any appliances we hadn't already mentioned?*

At 11:15, the fire captain declared the area safe and two men and a woman began combing through the wreckage of the store. They worked their way inside, taking even more photos and assessing the damage.

At 12:30, Jade and I were allowed to walk through the back door in the alley and see the inside for the first time.

Just as we'd been told, thankfully, most of the damage was from smoke and wasn't structural. There was modest water damage to the books nearest the front of the store and some blackened paint and charred shelving.

We tried to convince each other how blessed we were. The air was thick with the smells of stained memories. But they were not gone.

When we walked out of the front door, now an awkward opening without a door to close behind us, we saw my mother in conversation with Miles and Kendra.

Kendra ran to us and she wrapped her arms around Jade. "Oh my gosh, oh my gosh, are you guys OK? This is terrible. I don't know what to say at all. Oh my gosh, this is like a dream."

Jade patted her on the back and tried to nonchalantly pull away. "We're fine, sweetheart, no need to worry anymore."

Kendra moved to me. "Would it be OK to hug you?" she asked.

"Of course." I hugged her and thanked her for her concern.

I looked over her and saw Miles still standing next to my mother; the two remained engaged in discussion. I waved at Miles.

He waved back.

I excused myself and joined their conversation.

Miles revealed having heard of the fire from Kendra, who heard from another girl on the cheerleading squad, who heard from her uncle who'd driven her to her job at the mall, who was dating a 911 operator.

"I'm glad you found out, but I would have called you anyway, Miles."

"Thanks, Mr. C. I feel sick standing here looking at it."

I turned sideways and put my arm around him. "Me too, Miles."

We faced the shell of Paper Gems.

"How'd it start anyway?"

I shook my head and my mother inched closer. "I don't know yet, Miles. They're investigating that."

Miles shook his head, too, but not apparently at anything I'd said. "Crazy weird, right?"

"Crazy weird."

The elderly owner of the restaurant across the mall called from her doorway. "Cole, I have something for you."

I said good-bye to Miles and left him again with my mother.

The neighbor presented me with a kiss on the cheek and a pound cake. She offered her office if we needed it and use of her storage room.

I offered my thanks and assured her that if we needed either of them, I'd call. As I tried to leave, she offered each of the same conveniences yet again, plus use of her phone, fax machine, and grandson.

When I returned to the store, I noticed Mother now talking to the woman with the twin bichon frise puppies. She called Jade and Kendra over to say hello.

I noticed Miles standing in front of the store with his hands on his hips. He spun in a slow circle as if imagining where the door used to be. He ran his hand along the charred door frame and stepped gingerly through the rubble to the remains of a thick book.

He bent over and pulled it from a pile of ash. Then he asked one of the most surprising questions of the fall.

"Can I keep this?"

"Really?"

"Yeah."

"Why?"

"I dunno. Seems right. A memento, I guess."

"A souvenir."

He dropped his head. "I didn't mean it like that."

"I know you didn't, Miles. Yes, you can keep it."

He examined the book before replying. "Cool. Thanks, Mr. C. Sorry about your store."

"It was *our* store, Miles. Not just mine."

He looked up at me and said it again. "Cool."

Strangely, that time it meant more.

The remainder of the afternoon seemed to move in frames, like a graphic novel I never wanted to read.

An investigator sat with Jade and me in his car and asked about our enemies. "We have none," we both answered.

Our insurance agent came by with pizza and a claim form.

Candace and Jade's two part-time employees came to tell her they didn't need their next checks right away.

Mr. Buhl, principal at AHS, came by with a poinsettia. "I didn't know what to get that would say how sorry I am."

My office manager and five employees stopped by with enough supplies to clean up a fire at the Mall of America. "Don't worry, we'll take it out of your check." She winked. All of them gave me a hug, told me how grateful they were no one was hurt, and lamented the damage to the store they knew we loved.

Sometime after 5:00, the circus on the mall packed up and began moving on.

Jade and I sat on a bench with our backs to the store. She rested her head on my shoulder.

"Did this really happen?" Her voice was soft and sleepy.

"It did." I stroked her hair and pulled out an inch-long sliver of wood.

"What now?"

"We go home."

She sat up. "I mean *after* tonight."

"Oh. We clean up, I suppose."

Her expression suggested I go another step.

"I'm sorry, honey." I was, quite literally, having a hard time keeping my eyes open. "We wait for answers and rebuild. We move on. We thank the stars the place is still standing. The guy from the restoration place says if we hire them, they can have the store clean in a few days."

"What if they don't find the answers?"

"They will."

She took my hands and looked at the store simultaneously.

My eyes followed hers.

Her eyes remained locked on the black wreckage with the occasional white page peeking out. "Arson. Can you believe it? I . . . I don't even know what I should be feeling right now. I can barely say the word."

"We don't know that yet, not with certainty."

"But if it was. What then?"

I took a deep breath and prepared for what I'd predicted was coming hours ago.

"Then they find out who and why. It could have been random.

It could have been an old disgruntled client of mine. A prank gone wrong. A dare. Who knows. And maybe we'll never know."

"Cole, sweetheart, if we *never* know, I'll *never* sell another book in that store."

Just as I'd feared.

"We'll get the answers, Jade. We will."

"And if we don't find them, Paper Gems is history."

Just as I'd feared.

Jade stood up and stretched her arms high over her head.

I did the same and wiped ash and dirt off my pants.

Jade began walking toward the car, then stopped abruptly and turned around. "Sometimes the answers are easier than we think, Cole."

THIRTY-SEVEN

Recovery Day

JADE AND I SLEPT UNTIL 11:15 THE NEXT MORNING.
Neither of us could remember sleeping that long since our
college *recovery* days. *Recovery* from the all-nighters that were
such a part of our lives, but as thirtysomethings left us feeling
shredded and hollow-legged.

We enjoyed toaster waffles and were reminded that our water
heater doesn't hold quite enough for back-to-back showers. Jade
stepped out of the shower, cursed me, the water heater, or both,
and slipped into her thick cotton robe. She found me in the sitting room watching a report on the noon news about our fire.

"That's the store," Jade said.

"Uh-huh."

She sat next to me on the coffee table. Just as she asked,
"What are they saying?" the WVIR story ended and the local
weatherman took over.

I turned off the set. "Nothing new, mostly just a rehash of last night's piece."

"They say it was arson?"

"No, dear. Just that they're looking at it. I promise you. We won't hear it from Channel 29. We'll be the first to know."

Jade returned to the bedroom, dressed, blow-dried her hair, skipped the makeup, and asked me to take her to Paper Gems. "I need to see it again."

A half hour later I dropped her off and, after asking for the tenth time if she was sure she wanted to be alone, kissed her good-bye across the emergency brake.

"Let me know how it goes, please?"

"What?"

"Whatever happens next." She kissed me again and was gone.

My first stop was by the office. The office manager greeted me with, "Hey, boss, here to put out a few fires?"

I'd never seen a face turn more ashen with such speed.

"I'm sorry," was all she could muster.

It was plenty.

I returned a client phone call, called the power company and asked them to reconnect us as soon as possible, logged into my brokerage account and checked on my own portfolio, called my attorney, and called my insurance agent.

Then I promised myself once again not to take for granted how well the firm runs when I'm not around.

I called my mother. She was showing a home and would call back soon.

I called Principal Buhl to thank him again for the plant and visit.

I wrote a personal thank-you and a large check to the local Red Cross and asked my office manager to get it there.

I got back in my car and drove it through Express Car Wash. It didn't need the full treatment, but I let them vacuum it anyway.

I decided that Jade needed me whether she knew it or not. I also needed to see the store again. I drove down the alley and noticed the yellow police tape was gone. With rested eyes and more balanced judgment, I decided the cleanup would be easier than we'd originally judged. *No need to hire the fire restoration guys*, I thought.

I found Jade inside the store and put my arm around her without saying anything. I could only marvel at how we'd escaped complete loss. From the counter back, the store smelled like smoke and would need new paint. But nothing more.

Just when I was about to comment on our good fortune, Jade burst into tears. "It's a disaster," she said, then fell into nearly silent sobs.

"It's not as bad as it looked last night. I expected the whole place to be gutted. Look, even the furniture and decorations in the Reading Corner survived."

"You're right. It's not as bad as it looked last night. It's worse."

"Huh?"

"Paper Gems isn't about the furniture or the pictures on the wall or the shelves." She gestured toward the back. "It's not about stupid reindeer. It's about the *Gems*. And it looks like nearly half of the books were ruined by the very men who saved your precious wicker chair."

I walked to a shelf and looked at it with newly informed eyes. The books were swollen and deformed. Before I could think better of it I said, "They'll dry, won't they?"

The words came with a look. "They'll dry, all right. Like prunes. We could probably get two dollars for the lot at the recycling place."

I thought about the journals. Most of them were safe in Jade's office but the ones we had been reading most recently were still under the chair. I walked back to the corner and learned that the furniture wasn't exactly fine, after all. My chair and the stools could probably be salvaged but the love seat and sofa were soaked. So were the journals. I pulled them out and went back to Jade.

"The books may be ruined but at least some of the *Gems* are intact." I opened the wet journal and pointed to an entry. It had run a bit and some of the page behind showed through, but it could be read.

It *would* be read.

THIRTY-EIGHT

Rex's Journal

September 6, 1971

It's Labor Day again. I try to imagine how twelve months have gone by so fast. All those days. I don't feel like the person I did a year ago. Some of me feels better, some worse. But all of me feels older. Sometimes I feel older than my dad.

Sparks got angry with me today. I called her and said I wanted to go out to the lake today to say I was sorry again and maybe say a prayer. But she didn't think it was a good idea. She said we could take some flowers to the cemetery, but that she didn't want to spend all day thinking about it.

I told her that was fine and we said we'd meet later after work. I went to A&P and worked my shift, but the whole time I was thinking about Flick. I saw a little girl and her brother, I think it was her brother, come shopping with an older lady. I bet it was her grandma by the way she was talking to them.

The girl looked exactly like Flick. Not exactly, I guess, but close. I don't know how old she was, but I think probably eight.

I was bagging at line 3 when they came through. The girl wanted a pack of NECCO Wafers but her grandma wouldn't get them. The boy, he was younger for sure, he stuck his tongue out at her.

I was surprised the girl didn't cry or jump up and down. But she was sad. I could see it. So could the checker. I wanted so bad to buy her a pack and give it to her, but I guess I just didn't think of it fast enough. The lady wrote a check and they went out to the lot.

I just kept watching the whole time, feeling so sad for the girl. I wondered where her mom was.

After they left I told the checker, her name is Paje and she's older too, I told her how bad I felt. She told me not to worry about it so much. That's what adults have to do sometimes and that she says no to her kids a lot. Then she told me to go to the back and get more paper bags.

I made a promise that if the little girl came again when I was working that I would give her a pack of NECCO Wafers. I even bought a pack during my break and put them in my locker in the break room.

After my shift was over, I was going to pick something up at Jefferson Engraving but decided to go by the lake first. I know I had told Sparks I wouldn't, but it was like my car just went there. I sat on the edge of the lake close to where Flick died and I cried. Hardest I've cried in a long time I think.

I don't really know what time it was but Sparks came driving up in her mom's car. I saw her come through the lake entrance and across the bridge and I did everything I could to wipe everything off my face. But my eyes were puffy and my nose would not stop running for anything.

Sparks parked and walked down to the beach area where I was sitting. I sort of pretended like I didn't see her, but she knew I did. She didn't sit down at all. She reached her hand out and helped me up. Then she said she loved me and she wanted me to stop.

At first of course I figured she meant to stop crying. But she started getting upset at me. Like it was about more than that. Like I needed to stop feeling so sorry for myself all the time and thinking about it every day. She said I was drowning just like Flick.

Stop stop stop stop this. She said she didn't want to watch this anymore. She's not coming back, Rex. She's not going to come out of the water out there and play Frisbee again, Rex. She's dead and gone and she's not coming back. It's time to face it, Rex.

Sparks was yelling and crying at the same time. I'd never seen her do that before. It made me feel even worse.

After a while we left her car there and drove together to the cemetery. Sparks apologized and said she didn't mean to yell. She just wanted to get on with her life and wanted me to get on with mine. Her stepdad, Flick's real father, had packed up and left and her mom was sad all the time. Sparks said she needed one person she could talk to or ride with who wasn't always stuck on the sadness.

Sparks yelled at me today and I'm glad she did. It helped me. It made me think about someone else for a change.

THIRTY-NINE

Sparks's Journal

September 7, 1971

My sister died one year ago today. I couldn't even have written that short of a sentence about her a few months ago. Rex and what he's calling his daily Seventeen Second Miracles are spilling into my family's life and making it easier to move on. It's funny because he was in such bad shape at first that I was helping him. Now it's the other way around.

Usually I write about stuff that Rex tells me about that he doesn't put in his journal. This is one of those times I get to write about something I saw firsthand.

Mom still hasn't forgiven Rex. She and Rex are the only ones who still hold him responsible. At least, they're the last ones who are so bitter about it. Mom still cries over Flick's picture when she thinks nobody is looking. She's not ready to be friends with Rex again. At least not until today.

We stayed away from any Labor Day activities yesterday. We tried to make it just like any other day. I lied to my mom and went to the lake in the evening because I knew Rex would go there after work. That's all described in my diary. This is about Rex and what he did.

Today was our day to visit the lake and the cemetery as a family. Mom didn't want to deal with other people so we left real early in the morning, like 6:00. She and I were already crying before we even turned off 29.

Mom drove real slow to the beach. It was still pretty dark but the moon and glow of dawn made it possible to see OK. When we got to where it happened, I saw something glowing in the water.

We got out of the car and walked to the beach. Way out where Sis died was a metal bowl floating with a fire in it. It must have been anchored to the bottom somehow because it didn't move. It stayed right where she drowned. Nobody said anything. We just stood there for a few minutes, then got in the car.

When we got to the cemetery, we saw another bowl—it looked bronze or something—sitting on the grave. It was full of camp fuel and burning with a beautiful orange-and-blue flame. Engraved on the bowl was the word Flick.

Mom never talked about it but that was the day she started softening toward Rex. It must have been really hard for him to get both of those bowls in place before we got there. I can't think of anything else he could have done that would have touched Mom that way.

FORTY

Fathers

SHE'D DONE THE BEST SHE COULD.

The ranch-style house was in poor condition, but Beth Nielson had her own ideas about how best to shield the home from ridicule and her son from teasing at school. In the three months they'd been living in the area, she had planted along both sides of the small home and dotted the grass and flower beds with gnomes she'd bought at yard sales and craft fairs.

She had at least a dozen wind chimes hanging from the gutters on either side of the front door. They looked homemade; most of them bent forks and spoons strung together by what I guessed was most likely fishing line.

The ramp consisted of two sheets of plywood resting on four-by-eights and ran right over the three stairs in a straight line between the small concrete patio and the driveway. It was obvious the door wasn't wide enough for Travis's chair to pass, and I grimaced at imagining the contortions they must have to undergo daily to get Travis in and out.

The van was positioned at an odd angle in the driveway, front wheels on the grass, so that Travis's side door opened near the bottom of the ramp.

I walked up the ramp and rang the doorbell. A dog with a deep, intimidating bark began yelling at me from inside. A moment later, Beth shouted down the dog and opened the door.

Her face flushed instantly. "Mr. Conner."

"Hi, Beth. Is this a bad time?"

She kicked the growling dog back into the house. "Travis, call Wrigley, *please*."

I did not see him, but I heard Travis bark even louder for the dog to abandon his front-door vigilance.

"I'm sorry," she said when the door was shut behind her.

"Quite all right, Beth. I love dogs."

"Not *that* one," she said and brushed dog hair off her legs. "I'm also real sorry about the bookstore. I was shocked to hear about it. Good thing nobody was in there."

"We're all very grateful. The damage wasn't as bad as it looks on TV. We'll be able to open it back up sooner than we thought."

"That's good."

I flicked the end of the closest wind chime, an upside metal spatula with four sporks tied through the slits in big fishing line loops. "These are so creative."

"Thank you. They're different."

"They help add flavor, they really do." I tapped the bottom of another.

"That's nice of you," she replied, and I noticed her eyes finding an overturned box of aluminum cans in the yard. "It's not much to see here, I'm afraid."

"Nonsense."

She patted down some unruly hair on top of her head. "So . . . today really isn't good for a visit. I wish you'd called."

"You're right. I should have, and I apologize. I just wanted to say hello in person and meet with your son face-to-face."

Beth looked up and down the street, checked her watch, then double-checked the street again. "My ex-husband will be coming by again today to visit Travis, and, uh, I'm afraid I don't know when."

"Oh."

"You knew then?"

I shook my head. "No, no, only that he's been . . . away."

"Away in jail," she clarified.

"I see."

"He's been out for a week, this time anyway, and he's in town. He's been trying to come by every day to see Travis."

"That's nice," I said, having absolutely no idea what else I could possibly say.

She looked to the street again. "You know, it's early still. I'm guessing he won't come by for a while yet. I'll get Travis. I can't promise he'll come out. He's still pretty upset about that last meeting." Her eyes narrowed almost imperceptibly. "I was a little upset myself, but we're kind of used to it."

Between the convict husband, the vicious dog, the angry teenager, and the offended mother, I wasn't sure whether to thank her or race to my car. I considered both and did neither.

"I'll get him," she offered.

Before I could reconsider escaping, the front door opened again and Beth carried through Travis's partially collapsed wheelchair. She opened it up again on the raised concrete patio that ran the length of the house and bent over to lock the wheels.

I watched intently as she stepped back through the front door and into the living room. Travis sat on the edge of the plaid couch. His legs draping lifelessly over the edge, his feet sitting like lumps on the floor.

She turned around, crouched down, and he climbed onto her back.

She reached her arms around his upper body, stood, and carried him sideways through the door. Then she turned again and lowered him.

It was an exercise they'd perfected.

Beth patted his arm and politely excused herself.

While I was thanking her, Travis was rolling his chair down the ramp.

I caught up at the opening of the driveway, not ten feet from the street.

He hadn't looked at me yet.

"How you been, Travis?"

He shrugged and I shrugged back. I'm not sure why.

"I'd like to apologize, again, for what happened last week."

"Uh-huh."

"I know it must have hurt."

"Uh-huh."

"Listen to me, Travis. No one was more surprised than I."

"Got that right," he muttered.

"Excuse me?"

He shifted his Miami Dolphins cap slightly off center in my direction.

I wondered if he'd hoped I'd notice.

"I mean I knew," he said.

"Knew what? And I like your cap, by the way. You have an impressive collection."

He ignored me, or pretended to.

"I knew no one would stop, Mr. Conner."

"You did?"

He looked at me, finally. "Been in this chair awhile, dude."

"Fair enough. But surely people *do* help you, right? It must happen a lot."

He took his cap off. "Sometimes, yeah, I guess it does. But I mostly notice when people don't."

Exactly, I thought.

Two cars passed in front of us, going in opposite directions.

"Miles was cool, though."

I smiled. "Yes. He was cool, wasn't he?"

We watched two joggers glide by, side by side, at a brisk pace.

"Can I ask you a question?"

"Guess so."

"You don't have to answer if you don't want to. Or if you're not ready."

He took his hat off and looked up at me. "How'd I hurt my legs?"

I don't think it mattered to him, but I was still glad he'd been the one to say the words, not me.

"I wasn't born this way."

"Oh."

"I had an accident while we were living in Little Rock. I was twelve."

I'm sorry, I thought but remained silent.

He touched his thighs. "I can feel that, sorta. But I haven't walked since then."

While Travis was quiet, perhaps considering what more to say, if anything, I spotted and grabbed a green fabric lawn chair leaning against a trash can. I opened it up and sat next to him.

Travis had put his hat back on. "I don't like talking about it really that much. You know what I'm saying?"

"Of course."

He wheeled forward a few inches, then back. Forward, then back again. "We lived in a nasty house outside of Little Rock. Lived in lots of nasty houses. This one here is our nicest, by far."

"It's a fine home. Your mom has done a lot with it."

"She tries to do whatever, you know, to help it look OK."

I began to wonder how the scene would unfold if Travis's father showed up as we sat like two best friends at the edge of the road, counting cars. Looking across the street, I couldn't help but notice that the Nielsons' home was smaller and in worse shape than the neighbors'. It was a humble, older neighborhood stretching for the middle of middle class.

The watch, I thought. "Before I forget, Travis, I think this is yours." I pulled his pocket watch from my pocket and handed it to him.

"No, no, no," he said, watching it dangle from the chain in the air between us. "I don't deserve it."

"Of course you do. It's your reminder. Every second counts, right? Better yet, every seventeen seconds count."

"But I haven't earned it yet."

"You will."

He took the watch from my hand and studied it a moment. Then, without looking up again, he began. "I was playing at the end of the driveway with my sister." Off came the hat and he rubbed his freshly buzzed head. "We were drawing with that chalk, sidewalk chalk my mom called it. You seen it?"

"Sure."

"We had a bucket of it. My sister and me liked to draw. Play tic-tac-toe, whatever. It was fun. My sister and me were kinda like best friends, I guess . . . Anyway . . . my dad and mom got into a fight, which they did a lot. Sometimes I think it was Dad's fault. Sometimes I think it was Mom's. That's what he said. And they yelled a lot. I mean *a lot.* He screamed so loud when he was drinking a lot that his voice sounded all scratchy the next day."

Travis took a breath and paused while a middle-aged couple passed by holding hands. They looked at us and smiled, but did not say hello.

"We were writing our names, I think. My sis was just learning that, like how to not make the letters backward. My dad was shouting and cursing and we'd been outside a long time that day. It scared my sister a lot, 'cause, you know, she was a little kid."

"Of course. It sounds like you are good big brother."

"Not really." Travis's voice cracked for the first time. "You have a sister?"

"No," I answered. "I wish I did."

"Me too," he mumbled and scratched at the armrests of his wheelchair for a moment before continuing. "While we were still playing, Dad came out of the screen door cussing loud, calling Mom a b— Sorry. He was calling her lots of names, really."

"It's OK, Travis."

"He slammed the door shut behind him and turned around and put his foot through the screen. No reason for it. No stupid reason for *any* of it." He let out a chestful of air.

"Take your time."

"He kept shouting all the way to the car, that old piece, his cheap Dodge. He got in, turned it on, and revved the engine extra loud, you know, like guys do sometimes."

"Uh-huh."

"Then my sister, Trista—I told you her name, right?"

With every sidebar it seemed he could successfully gather his emotions, at least momentarily.

"I think so, yes."

"We got out of the way real fast. Way onto the grass. Then my dad popped the car in reverse. Right then, Trista saw the bucket of chalk and went running over to grab it. Dumb girl just didn't want to see the bucket crushed, you know?"

"I know."

Travis grabbed at the front of his T-shirt.

"I didn't mean to call her dumb." As if flipping a switch, or pulling a trigger, all at once the tears came. "She wasn't dumb at all."

I stood up and pulled the chair away. I got on my knees next to him.

"She was so fast, she just got away from my hand so, so fast. She jumped out to get the bucket of chalk and he ran right over her. I started shouting at him but he didn't hear. I guess he just didn't hear. Trista was stuck under the car and he kept hitting the gas. I threw myself in there. I reached in to get her loose. But I slipped and he drove over my waist. Back tires, then front."

I put my arm around his shoulders and he covered his face and sobbed into his hat.

Through the layer of cotton he said, "My legs never moved again."

"I'm so sorry, Travis."

"And Trista was dead."

Then came the pain I knew Travis felt when I told Flick's story.

Then also came the silence.

FORTY-ONE

Drive

I DIDN'T DRIVE STRAIGHT HOME.

The first few miles away from Travis's home were spent being thankful his father had not arrived before I left.

The next stretch passed with me wondering how much his father had changed, if at all, and why he'd rushed back from a prison in Arkansas when his wife was no longer his wife.

Then I just worried about Beth and Travis.

As I drove the back roads of Albemarle County, I imagined the brutal fights Travis must have witnessed during his life, the brand of emotional warfare that turns physical, the words that no child should ever hear his parents shout at each other.

I was no stranger to fighting and as I crossed the James River I reflected on my first fight with Jade.

"What are we doing? It's our honeymoon," I told her. "No one fights on their honeymoon."

"We do when you don't put me first," she answered.

The words cut me then; in fact, they still cut me now. Just as the dispute was ridiculous then and is certainly ridiculous now.

Jade and I were on a seven-day cruise deep in the Caribbean. The weather and food were so ideal, so richly satisfying, it felt like we'd stepped through the TV and into a Sunday-morning infomercial. For the first time in my life, the colorful brochures and slick commercials had delivered exactly what we'd been promised.

We arrived at the French island of Martinique overnight and had the day to explore the island, snorkel, lie in the sand on the picturesque beaches, or spend money in the local shops and boutiques. Loud warnings from the captain and his mates sternly reminded us that the ship would not wait for latecomers.

After omelets and fresh juice on the ship, one of their promised seven meals and snacks a day, we disembarked and began enjoying a day on dry land. We rented cheap mopeds, the beginning of Jade's love for them, and enjoyed the island's personality.

We bought gifts for both our mothers, exquisite jewelry made by two shy women under a canopy.

Later we had our picture drawn together in pastels on a water-stained pad of paper by a toothless man in a folding chair. He was a gem, and the picture still hangs in our home today.

For a late lunch we ate seafood on a pier within view of the gargantuan ship that had carried us there. The chunky salsa and fish were as fresh as anything I'd ever tasted in my life. And I didn't even like fish back then.

After lunch we returned the mopeds and walked to the beach. Jade lathered my shoulders in powerful sunblock and I gladly returned the favor, covering her back, thighs, and arms. When I was done I suggested getting out of the sun in our cabin back on the ship, but she kicked sand on me and continued reading her book.

It was the kind of afternoon you dream of when life lies to you, when it teases you with a good morning but destroys it with a speeding ticket or afternoon bad news. You dream of days that begin at sea, unwind in the island sun, sand, and deep blue water, and end on the deck of a ship holding hands with a lover in deck chairs, wondering how many stars are in that little circle you draw with your finger in the sky above your head.

At some point, I dozed off on my chest. When I awoke, Jade had placed a towel over my back to keep me from burning. She was still right next to me, still smiling, still reading her book.

The ship's horn sounded and was so loud I told Jade our mothers must have heard it. We gathered our things, not in a rush, and began walking back toward the long pier that led to one of several entrances. Just before we stepped off the island for the last time, Jade spotted a boy selling necklaces with a single shark tooth, or what he said was a shark tooth. Jade patted him on the head, tussled his dark hair, and bought two.

She blew a kiss to the island and we began the long walk down the pier toward the ship. Couples just like us, couples with children, and older travelers walked alongside us in a parade of tired vacationers.

It was one of those senior cruise goers who caught my eye.

The woman, in her seventies I guessed, was standing against a rail with her fingers interlocked and her hands pulled tight against her chest. She wore long, modest paisley shorts, a silk Hawaiian-style shirt, sunglasses, and an oversized straw hat she might have purchased from one of a dozen vendors selling them near the port.

I didn't know her name, where she was from, even what language she spoke. The ship was filled with passengers from around the world. But I knew she was worried. Those looks are universal.

I'd passed her initially, but a lifetime of watching my father sent me back. "Ma'am, is there something wrong?"

She looked at me, but only for an instant, then her gaze turned back to the herds of people moving like cattle toward the ship. The numbers were thinning.

"Ma'am?"

She removed her sunglasses. "My husband isn't back yet."

"Oh," I said. "Well, I'm sure he'll make it."

"My gosh, I hope so."

"Can we wait with you?" Jade joined us.

"Oh no, you kids get on the ship. He'll be rightly along." Her words were the only confident thing about her. Her eyes and tone were increasingly fearful.

"Did you get separated?" I asked.

"Not at all, no. We got here together, but he asked me to wait here while he went back for something. I promised not to leave this spot."

I looked at Jade, then back at the woman. "How long ago?"

"Half an hour, maybe. Gosh, I don't know."

Jade put her hand on the woman's arm. "I'm sure he'll be back soon. Right, honey?"

"Right." With my finger, I motioned Jade to follow me. We took five steps toward land and I stopped her. "What if he doesn't make it back? What if something has happened to him?"

We both looked at the flow of passengers. It had slowed even more.

I checked my watch. It was 5:15, just fifteen minutes until the final departure horn.

"He'll be fine, honey. He's probably at one of the street vendors right there." She pointed to shore.

"Maybe." I returned to the woman.

"Would you like me to go back down there and look for him?"

"I . . . I don't want you to do that."

"I'd be happy to. I'd hate for him to be left behind, it's a long swim back."

The woman laughed awkwardly.

"Honey," Jade whispered in my ears. "He'll make it back. They have people to help with this kind of thing."

It was my turn to put my mouth to her ear. "She's terrified, dear. I'll just run down there, very fast, as fast as I can, and make sure he's coming. Make sure nothing's happened."

Again we switched places and she added in a whisper, "This isn't your job, honey. Let the ship handle it if he's any later. But he's fine. You know he's fine. Please don't go."

Before she could move her head, I whipped around and kissed her on the lips. Then I turned my attention back to the woman. "What does he look like, ma'am?"

"You don't—"

"What does he look like?" I pushed the way I'd seen my father push.

"He's quite short, shorter than I. And he's wearing a shirt like this, but not exactly the same, but the hat he's wearing is a big one just like this." She grabbed the brim as if to demonstrate its size. "His name is Gerry with a G."

I pulled my own sunglasses off my head, handed a shopping bag to Jade, and said, "I'll be right back."

I took a peek at Jade's expression before racing away. I thought, *If looks could kill, this is going to be a very short marriage.*

Back onshore I scanned in all directions for a short man in a Hawaiian shirt with a giant hat. A ship employee shouted at me, "Sir, are you boarding the ship?"

"Yes, I'm just looking for someone."

"The ship will leave, sir, as scheduled. Please board."

I held up both hands. "Please, just one minute. See? Look around, there are still others coming." There were a few stragglers making their way to the pier, but it was now just a trickle.

I ran toward a row of street vendors. "Gerry? Gerry?" There were still so many tourists from other ships on other itineraries and it appeared they'd all bought the same hat. "Gerry?"

Nothing.

I looked back at the pier at the backs of the last passengers walking toward the ship. Someone was flapping her arms in my general direction. *Jade.*

I began to jog down the street. "Gerry? Is there a Gerry from that ship?"

Locals and tourists mostly ignored me and carried on. Three minutes in one direction, three minutes in another.

"Gerry?" I called again and could sense the early taste of panic.

The horn blew its final, long, bold warning. As the sound died across the ocean, I saw a man walking up a side street toward me in a colorful shirt and hat. He was carrying a flower. "Gerry?"

"Yes?" The man was out of breath and sweating much more than anyone in the commercials or brochures.

"I came to make sure you didn't miss the ship. Your wife was worried."

He panted and coughed. "Thank you." More coughing. "You didn't need to." More panting. "I wanted this." He held up a stunning yellow flower, one I'd never seen before.

"It's lovely."

"I saw it earlier and wanted to surprise her. I meant to go back, but I forgot."

We fast-walked together back to the ship. The same woman who'd implored me to board smiled as we passed.

Jade and Gerry's wife were waiting, one more patiently than the other, in the place we'd both left them.

Gerry handed his wife the flower and apologized for worrying her.

She wrapped her arms around him and kissed him. "You made it. I was so worried. It's a long swim back, you know."

He grinned at her.

Jade reminded us the ship was leaving and we hustled the rest of the way. Only a handful of ship employees boarded after us.

Back in the cabin, we changed for dinner and Jade reminded me how close I'd cut it. We found ourselves bickering like a couple married four decades, not four days.

I should have brought her a flower, too.

FORTY-TWO

Grateful

GRATEFUL.

That was how Jade and I felt during the cleanup. We'd elected to do most of it ourselves and both felt it had proven less difficult and the fire less damaging than we first thought.

There was kill-staining and painting to be done, something recommended to help with the smoke smells, but that was hired out and scheduled for the next day. Professionals were also coming to repair the front doors and all the glass. We vacuumed, mopped, and waxed all the floors. The ancient hardwood floors had so many coats of lacquer on them that they survived being wet without warping. The large rug in the Reading Corner along with the love seat and sofa had to be replaced but the other furniture was fine.

The damage to the books was extensive, but not as bad as Jade had initially thought. She must have picked a shelf that had been directly in the path of the powerful fire hose. Books on other shelves were either completely dry or salvageable. Jade even managed to make a joke about her upcoming Christmas Fire Sale.

The real financial damage wasn't in the lost books—insurance would cover that—it was in the Christmas shopping money we wouldn't see. Just like most retail businesses, Paper Gems made most of its profit between Thanksgiving and New Year's. This would be a lost year for Jade in more ways than one.

"You never told me how it went," she commented after a long lull.

"How what went?"

"Yesterday. At Travis's house."

"Oh. Well, you never asked."

"I didn't think I had to." She pulled a new set of dishrags from a Target bag and ripped them out of the paper sleeve.

"I didn't meant it like that, Jade." I took a clean rag from her. "It was hard. Travis has had a tough life and he shared some of it with me."

"I'm sure he has," she said with just a touch of bite in her voice.

I was considering whether the time was right to tell her Travis's story when she preempted me with a question. "Did you ask him?"

"Ask him what?"

"About the fire."

"I didn't think I had to."

She didn't appreciate the wordplay.

I wiped my hands off and put them on Jade's shoulders. "He didn't have anything to do with it."

How do you know? her expression asked.

"Jade, for one, he doesn't drive, and his mother didn't bring him into town to torch your store. And for two, it's not in him."

It was hard to gauge whether Jade was embarrassed or dubious.

"How do you know?"

Dubious.

"Think about it, sweetheart. Did someone else drive his van? They borrowed it from Beth? Or did he post an ad on Craigslist looking for an accomplice with a wheelchair-equipped vehicle?"

I turned her around and wrapped my arms around her waist. "Whoever did this, I just know, I just know it wasn't Travis."

"Then who?"

I squeezed her tight. "I don't know, but they're still working, I guarantee you that. Plus it's only been three days."

"I suppose you're right."

I let that hang between us. Not because I needed to be right, but because I didn't want to fill the space with words and risk sounding like I was gloating.

She kissed my forearm and spun around inside my arms to face me. "It could have been worse, right?" She put her hands on my upper arms.

"That's right."

"We could have lost it all and I need to feel more grateful. I know I do."

"Easier said, sweetheart. Easier said."

FORTY-THREE

Porch Furniture

WHERE WILL WE MEET?

The thought hit me like a stone column as we drove home. "I've got to have furniture for tomorrow."

"Tomorrow?"

"For the Discussion."

"You're going ahead with it?"

"Of course I am. You thought we wouldn't?"

"I didn't know." She paused. "That's why I asked."

With my eyes on the road and one hand on the wheel, I unplugged my cell phone from the car charger and handed it in Jade's direction. "Would you call Cami at the office?"

She scrolled through the phone book. "Why?"

"Her husband has a nice rig, a Ford dually. I want to see if I can borrow it."

"What for?"

"A trip to Lowe's, Schewels, and Michaels."

When the phone began to ring, Jade handed it to me and picked her purse off the floor. It took less than sixty seconds to get access to the truck for the night and her fourth or fifth *I'm sorry* since the fire.

I asked Jade if she wanted to join me.

She declined. "How late will you be?"

"Not late."

I dropped her off in the driveway, thanked her for being understanding, drove to the office, picked up Cami's extra key, drove to her home in Forrest Lakes, switched rides. and drove to Lowe's. I bought a white wicker chair like the one at the store and two gas patio heaters. Then I went to the furniture store and bought the ugliest love seat I could find.

The last stop was Michaels at Barrack's Road. A short clerk in a green sweater with built-in bells approached.

"May I help you find something?"

I laughed at her name tag. "Sandi Clause?"

"The one and only."

She pointed out four Christmas displays on our way to an aisle crammed with holiday decor from floor to ceiling. "Can I get you anything else?"

"The biggest cart you've got."

"How about a sleigh?"

An hour later, I unloaded the haul in the driveway. It took yet another hour to put everything in place. I was relieved when a neighbor offered to make the task a little easier with an extra set of hands.

By the time we finished, the porch looked like something even Clark Griswold would have called gaudy and overdone.

As I put the space heaters on the lawn near opposite corners of the porch, I thought how ironic it would be if I torched the porch that was replacing our torched store.

My neighbor slapped me on the back, told me I was nuts, and returned home.

I moved to sit on the love seat but stopped myself. *Miles and Kendra should be first,* I thought.

Instead I sat in my new white chair and wriggled my rear until the cushion was comfortable.

It felt as close to normal as I'd known in four days. It felt as close to normal as I might know for the rest of the year.

A pizza delivery car raced by much too fast with a pizza slice strapped to the top of the car.

A Snow's Garden Center truck also passed and I sent a text message to Jade reminding her that we might want to have them replace the shrubs in the big concrete planters that had been damaged.

ME: We should call Snows about plants at Gems

JADE: OK

ME: U OK?

JADE: Yes be home soon

ME: Returning truck

JADE: OK

ME: U OK?

JADE: Yes just need u—am lonely—scared
ME: OK
JADE: Bring ice cream
ME: :-)

I did as I was asked. I returned the truck, thanked Cami and her husband, Nick, gave them twenty dollars for gas—they refused to take until I balled it up and chucked it in the door as it shut behind me—and stopped at Giant for ice cream.

Then I called a client on a whim to see if she'd open her flower shop for me. Jennifer and her husband lived in a house next door to a quaint downtown flower shop that was more pet project than profitable business venture.

Jennifer met me at the shop and sold me three dozen roses in three separate vases. I wrote on three mini cards, stuck each one in a separate envelope, and attached them to holders tucked into each arrangement.

She hugged me good-bye, said she was sorry about the shop, and walked me out. When I got home, I opened the door to find Jade curled up on the couch watching *Titanic* on AMC.

It took two trips to get the three vases of roses and set them on the coffee table in front of her.

I set the third one next to the others and handed her one pint of ice cream, Chubby Hubby, and kept the other, Cake Batter, for me.

She sat up, and with two spoons from the kitchen I joined her on the love seat facing the TV.

She didn't say anything and neither did I.

We didn't need to.

We ate ice cream and watched as the *Titanic* hit an iceberg, Jade leaned into my arm and whispered, "You know how this ends, right?"

"The movie or the date?"

"Both."

I lightly tapped the end of her nose with my spoon. "Just open your cards. Any order you like."

She tore open the first. "You."

Then the second, "I."

Finally, the third, "Love."

FORTY-FOUR

One-on-One

"**SORRY I'M LATE.**"

I looked at my watch, even though I'd looked at it every two minutes for the last half hour and I knew exactly what time it was: 5:45 P.M. "It's no problem, Kendra. I'm glad you're here. I was afraid you hadn't gotten word of our move to the house." I stood from the chair I'd been in since 5:00.

Kendra spun around and with her keychain set the alarm on the silver Audi she'd parked on the street in front of my house.

"Nice car," I said.

"Thanks."

"Lucky girl."

"Not really." She put the keys in her purse and set it on a chair. "Where's Travis?"

"Good question."

Kendra looked at my sad attempt to re-create the Reading Corner. "It's so weird, Mr. C."

"That's one way to put it." I reclaimed my seat.

"Is your wife home?" She was still standing and mustering a smile.

"She's not. She's working at the store today."

Her smile softened. "Oh."

"Did you want to talk to her? I could call."

"No bother. Next time maybe." Kendra's attention moved to the new love seat. "You put a love seat on your porch?"

I smiled. "I did. We couldn't have the Discussions without the love seat. Not having the Reading Corner is bad enough."

"You're funny."

I pointed at it. "You know, Kendra, I hoped you and Miles would be the first to sit in it, to officially christen it. Is he coming?"

Kendra turned her back on the love seat and sat across from me in one of the other three chairs. "I don't care."

"Don't know or don't care?"

"Both."

"I'm sorry to hear that."

"Yeah."

"You want to talk about it?"

"Not really."

"Up to you."

We sat quietly and listened to the hiss of the patio heater.

"So, Kendra, do you think the boys didn't think we'd meet today?"

"Why?"

I cocked my head and raised one eyebrow.

"The fire. Duh. Yeah, that could be."

"Should we call?" I already had my cell phone and their numbers at the ready. "Should we make sure they got the message?"

She shrugged and pulled at the thread in a factory-manufactured hole in her jeans.

"I'm just tired of it."

"Of what?"

"I dunno. All of it, I guess."

"The Discussions?"

"No! I love coming and learning about you and your dad. I didn't mean that at all."

"Then what?"

She sighed in the tender way only a seventeen-year-old with the entirety of the world's troubles on her shoulders can. "Miles. My dad. Basketball. Being a kid."

I crossed my legs and put my cell phone in my shirt pocket. "Hmm."

"Can you keep a secret?"

I scanned the porch with huge eyes and bent down to look under my chair. "Coast is clear, yes."

She whispered, "I hate cheerleading."

"You hate being a cheerleader? You're captain of the squad."

She put a finger to her pursed lips. "I know. And I hate it. I always have."

"So why do it all these years?"

"Because I'm not supposed to hate it. It's supposed to be in my blood. Cheerleading, honor roll, SCA, just like my mother."

"I see."

"Want to know another secret?"

I didn't have time to answer.

"I didn't even sign up. *He* did. He signed me up in the eighth grade. I had tried out for the girls YMCA basketball team and he told me I couldn't do it. But that I could do cheerleading if I wanted. And he said I wanted."

"So you did."

"Uh-huh. And I was good at it. I'm super athletic. Just like him."

"Why not tell him? Why not just say you don't care for cheerleading anymore?"

Kendra's gaze appeared to be fixed on the love seat. "You don't know my dad very well, do you?"

"I don't, no."

"He is . . . very . . . I don't know . . . very . . . *demanding.*"

"Of you?"

"Sort of, but not really. More of Miles. If that makes any sense."

Not really, I thought. "Go on."

"My dad wants to win. Basketball games, trophies, golf matches."

And arguments? I thought.

"When you were a kid, Mr. C., did you ever feel like you couldn't please your dad?"

I laughed out loud. "Sure I did. That's not uncommon at all. Sometimes parents put pressure on kids and it seems like we can't get things right. But they still love us. And they're proud of us."

"I guess."

"Kendra, my dad expected me to be just like him from the very beginning, right from birth. Shoot, he probably expected me to personally thank the doctor for his efforts with a box of Godiva chocolates when I came out."

She giggled.

"But I just wasn't like him. It took time, a lot of time. I learned as I grew up I'd never be my father; I had to accept I could only be an improved version of how I saw myself. But if I had one wish now, now in my old, grey, and fat days, it would be to be a perfect reflection of him."

She looked away. "Not me. That would never be me."

"Why?"

"For starters, because my dad doesn't want me to be like him. But he doesn't want me to be like my mom either. She's a 'floater,' he says. He wants me to be better, smarter, have a better resume, more opportunities—you know, all that stuff. Get straight A's, go to college, marry Miles, who he loves like his own kid, I think. Sometimes I think he'd pick Miles over me if he had to."

"That's not true, Kendra."

Kendra looked at the love seat again. "We both know why he isn't here, Mr. C."

She was right.

I knew it.

And she knew *I* knew it.

"But *you're* here," I said. "And why? Do we know yet why you were invited to attend these Discussions?"

"Not really. I like coming, I definitely like coming."

"What have you learned?"

"Lots of stuff. About your dad and the little girl. About loving other people."

I asked, faking puzzlement, "We've talked about that?"

"Sure we have. All those things your dad did for people and all the things they did for him. The daily miracles."

I took to my feet. "I don't have the hot chocolate–making skills of Jade but I can microwave water and add Swiss Miss. Can I bring you a mug?"

"Awesome, yeah, thank you."

I went into the house and into the kitchen. While the water got hot, I grabbed two hot chocolate packets, two Little Debbie Star Crunches, and one of my father's journals.

We checked the temperature of our drinks and Kendra closely examined her Star Crunch. "I've never had one of these."

"They're made in heaven."

She squeezed it until one of the ends popped open. "Why not."

After we finished them—mine in three bites, hers in nine—I asked, "Can I read you something?"

FORTY-FIVE

Rex's Journal

February 13, 1989

Sometimes people are so kind that I cannot keep track of it all. Today is such a day and only a list does the miracles justice.

SEVENTEEN SECOND MIRACLES I EXPERI- ENCED TODAY:

I was late to work and Daniel held the elevator for me when I knew he was already late, too.

I got a postcard from my sweetheart today. No reason, just because.

Two people stopped me in the mall today and asked me if I was Rex Conner from the radio. They said they loved my show and the stories I tell. They didn't have to do that.

Eric Garman from the theater that's been sponsoring the first hour of my show called me today to apologize for not returning my call yesterday when he'd promised to. Who does that anymore?

Who apologizes for something so simple as not returning a phone call? Eric Garman does, and I was so impressed I told him so.

Cole and I had an argument on Friday and we have not spoken much. I fear I pushed him away. That does not make me proud! Then today he asked how my day was when he got home from school and I was here already. He broke the ice, just like that. He knew just what he was doing by starting a simple discussion. Amazing kid. I admit I'm not a good dad all the time. But he's a good kid. All the time.

FORTY-SIX

Practice

I HADN'T HEARD FROM TRAVIS AND I'D LEFT THREE MES-
sages. I resisted the urge to drive out again and risk a run-in
with his father.

There was still no news on the cause of the fire. They suspected arson, but they had no hard evidence of either a crime or
a perpetrator. I suspected that this wasn't their most pressing case.

Over my strenuous objections, they'd looked at Travis because
of his reputation at school and his father's criminal record. They
also looked into a woman from the station who claimed I had
her fired, and Marci Wright, my client under the stress of an
IRS audit. They'd talked less seriously to another ten to fifteen
people in my circle of daily life.

Jade worked long hours both days and still felt behind. While
she'd grown increasingly upset that the fire remained a mystery,
she buried herself in getting Paper Gems ready to reopen. We

would still miss most of the Christmas shopping season but anything would be better than nothing.

The repainting of the store was done; besides some lingering paint fumes, for all practical purposes, the store itself was ready for books again. In fact, though I kept the observation to myself, Paper Gems actually looked better than the day it opened.

The real work was in going through all the books, deciding what could be saved and sold at full price, what could be sold "as is," and what was completely lost.

I hadn't told Jade yet, but restocking the store was going to happen no matter what. I'd replace every book out of my own pocket if I had to and fight the insurance company later. The distributor Jade used most had promised to send any books other stores refused and reorder the rest once the Christmas rush was over.

TRAVIS WASN'T THE ONLY ONE IGNORING MY CALLS. I'D called Miles Monday after Kendra left, Tuesday morning before school, and Tuesday *during* school. I'd even sent text messages, but he'd not been courteous enough to reply.

On Tuesday afternoon, I texted Kendra and asked if the varsity team was practicing after school. She called me during a break.

"Today's actually their first Tuesday practice. They have a scrimmage Thursday."

"Are you two better?" I posed.

"Better?"

"Speaking."

"Yeah, I guess. Dad, Coach, whatever, he made me invite Miles over to dinner."

"I see." I'd known I was going to ask anyway, but hearing they were on speaking terms again made it much easier. "Will you do me a favor?"

"Sure I will."

"Will you meet me there?"

"School?"

"Yes."

Silence.

Phone shuffling.

More silence.

Awkward considering and reconsidering.

"Why?"

"I want to talk to you both."

"Can't it wait until tomorrow?"

"I think you know why we can't wait until tomorrow. If we do, it's going to be a party of three on my porch: you, me and Little Debbie."

Cue the dramatic sigh, I thought.

And there it was.

"OK, Mr. C. I'll do it. What time?"

"I'll be there when school ends."

WE MET BY THE DOUBLE DOORS LEADING INTO THE ALBE-marle High School gym.

We walked in and sat on the mostly empty bleachers watching the players run layup drills.

Miles spotted us immediately and waved coolly with a single finger.

Coach Max spotted us, too. And though he didn't sprint, he sure got to us fast enough.

"Can I help you?"

"Hi, Dad."

"Kendra, what's Mr. Conner doing here?"

"We wanted to talk to Miles."

"Have you lost your little mind? We're practicing."

I stepped off the bleachers. "Not now, Coach, of course. We meant after. We don't want to interrupt."

"Fine. Then wait someplace else. The old gym is open if you want to wait there. We'll be done in thirty."

Kendra jumped off the bleachers and thanked her father.

"Uh-huh," he said and walked away.

We walked back to the athletic wing at the back of the school and entered through a propped-open door. The doors to the older of the two gymnasiums at AHS were open and all the lights on. "Play a game of pig?" I asked as I walked toward a lone basketball in the corner of the gym.

"It won't be pretty for you," she said.

"We'll see." I sent the ball to her with a firm bounce pass. "You first."

She caught the ball and in one fluid motion shot from where she stood, about six inches inside the three-point line.

Swoosh.

As we played we debated politics, something I'd never allow during the Discussions. I couldn't hide how impressed I was with her knowledge of the issues.

"You might be the most knowledgeable class president in the world."

"Nah," she answered, "just the United States."

She admitted to having skipped school in late February to watch President Obama's much-ballyhooed health-care summit.

"You did what?"

"Yeah, I thought it was really interesting. But I watched the MSNBC coverage; it's way better than FOX."

She nailed a turnaround jumper from the left side of the key. I missed.

We shared opinions on all the commentators from Matthews to Cavuto, O'Reilly to Olbermann, and Beck to Maddow.

"How do you watch all these?" I asked.

"DVR. I catch up on the weekends if my homework is done."

"And your homework is—"

"Usually done. Yeah."

Just as the topic turned to Miles, my cell phone rang.

"Hey, sweetheart," I answered.

"Hi. Where are you?"

"School."

"Huh?"

"AHS."

"Uh-oh. They revoke your degree?"

"I wish. Have you been over here lately? It's really changed."

We continued bantering and Kendra whispered, "Is that Mrs. Conner?"

I nodded as Jade complained again about Paper Gems's landlord in my ear.

"Can I say hi?"

I nodded and added a big smile. "Hey, Jade, Kendra wants to say hi. All right?"

I handed the phone to Kendra and her face lit up. "Hi, Mrs. Conner . . . Waiting for Miles to get out of practice . . . The new gym . . . He did? I didn't know that . . . Can he dunk?"

I pointed at myself with both hands.

Kendra nodded and laughed.

Totally, I mouthed.

"OK, I guess . . ." Kendra's voice softened.

I continued listening to Kendra's side of the phone call, hearing only occasional cackles and random syllables from my wife.

"That sounds like a good one . . . Really? How many hours could I get? Awesome . . . Yeah . . . I'd have to ask, I'm not eighteen yet . . . I will, I promise . . . Ha . . . OK, I'll tell him . . . Here he is." She handed the phone back to me.

"You telling stories about me?" I said into the phone.

"Sorry, babe, girl secrets."

"That's what worries me."

Jade went quiet a second. "Honey, be careful."

"I will."

"Call me later?"

"Of course."

We said good-bye and I put the phone back in my pocket. "Your shot."

"Bank shot," she said and she drilled a seven-footer.

I missed.

"You're a P-I-G," she teased.

"Aren't all men?"

Kendra laughed and we walked to the bleachers and sat. "You know, she's a really cool lady, Mr. C."

"Yes, she is. The coolest."

She exhaled. "I hope I find that someday, too."

"You will."

"Maybe."

"Not *maybe*. You're wonderful and you'll find the right fit."

"I think I already have a fit."

"Miles?"

She nodded.

"You're not married to Miles, Kendra. You're seventeen years old."

"Tell my dad that. I never really had a choice. I do what Dad says. So does Miles."

"But you have feelings for him, obviously."

"He's the only boyfriend I've ever had, Mr. C. When we were freshmen I liked him like you check-a-box-and-pass-a-note like someone. And it became this." She paused again. "I want what you and your wife have. And what your dad and mom had."

"What about what your own mom and dad have?"

"Eh," Kendra mused.

I changed the subject back to politics, this time local, and we talked for another half hour.

Miles never came.

Eventually we moved back outside and Kendra apologized for Miles, which I didn't understand and assured her she didn't need to do. Then she thanked me for talking, told me to tell Jade she would go by the store soon, and drove off in her mother's Audi.

Concerned Miles may not have gotten the message, I returned to the school and entered the boys' locker room. Coach Max was sitting at his desk.

"Yes," he said without looking up from his clipboard.

"Did you happen to tell Miles we were waiting in the gym for him?"

"Of course I did, Mr. Conner."

"Huh. Interesting. He never came."

Coach looked up and took off an unflattering and oddly fitting pair of reading glasses. "I watched him walk in there, Mr. Conner. We came in together. Is there anything else?"

"No, sir. Thank you." I turned to leave. "Actually, there is." I faced him again. "Your daughter has quite a jump shot."

He didn't answer. In fact, he didn't even look up.

The next morning, Miles Bohn broke up with Kendra Wilson. No tears. No argument. No explanation.

FORTY-SEVEN

My Miracle

IT DIDN'T COME NATURALLY.

Dad's passion for small acts of service—his daily miracles— did not become part of my life as a child, teenager, or young adult. In fact, I often resented the impact it had on my life. It wasn't true, of course, but I sometimes wondered if he was rais- ing me seventeen seconds at a time. Maybe I was just another soul in need. By the time I left home, I accepted his life's work as important and worthwhile, but I was not inclined to follow in his footsteps. My service was more measured, considered, spread out, and, wherever possible, convenient.

Our relationship matured over time and I enjoyed sharing time with him as another adult. Mom was very pleased that my teen indifference had mellowed into an affectionate friend- ship. I still didn't go out of my way to emulate his "miracles," but I didn't cringe when he performed one when I was around. Sometimes I even joined in without resenting it.

When Jade came into my life, the Conner family dynamics changed again. My parents accepted my fiancée and then my wife with more than open arms. They practically adopted her. She and I were equal siblings as far as they were concerned, and that was just fine with me. Having a fourth person in the family seemed to completely remove any remaining awkwardness. The first four or five years of marriage were the happiest of my life up until then.

Life took another turn when Jade found out she couldn't have children. All at once, the issues that every normal couple ignores and stores up during the early years of marriage came spilling out.

She resented the fact that I got to live my life as planned while hers had to fit in around it. She expected to be a successful writer, a perfect mom, or both. The doctor told her she wouldn't be the latter. Many publishers and editors convinced her she wouldn't be the former.

I was upset that she wasn't satisfied with what she had. In my then-selfish mind, my wife didn't appreciate the sixty hours a week I put in so that she could have a nice house with a beautiful porch. It was the porch, in fact, that sent me to my dad.

"Jade, I'm really trying here. It's not my fault that things aren't going your way."

"See, that's what I mean. It's becoming about my way and your way. What about *our* way?"

"Oh, for goodness' sakes, is there anything I can say that won't get twisted into something I do wrong?"

"You just don't get it, Cole. We signed up for something together. *Together*, Cole. Not you and me each getting what happens to come our way. Cole and Jade, Jade and Cole, planning, working, loving, being a *family*."

I regretted the words before I even said them. "A family without children."

Jade banished me to the porch and I didn't argue. She began to call it *my* porch, as in, "Go chill on your porch, Cole," or, "Dinner's out on your porch."

Jade must have talked to Mom, who talked to Dad, who took me out for ice cream one afternoon. After some prodding, and it didn't take very much, I told him everything. I shared feelings I hadn't even revealed to Jade.

He listened.

When I ran out of things to say, I ended with, "I love her, Dad. What can I do? I don't want to lose her."

"You feel love for her, Son, but it doesn't sound like you *love* her very much."

I was more confused than angry at what he said. "What do you mean I don't love her? I love her more than anything."

"Love is a verb, Cole. Your mother and I have very strong feelings of attraction, romance, and loyalty. We also love each other."

I still didn't get it. "That's the same thing."

"When I do a little act of service for someone, for that moment, I love them. I often don't know anything about them and if I did, I might not like them at all. The act is love."

Thirty years of example clicked. I replayed in my mind some of the times Dad "dragged me along" on his Seventeen Second Miracles. He wasn't being goody-goody, he was just being good. Loving others helped him forget himself, and forgetting himself, taking focus away from his own needs and wants, helped him learn to love others, including me and Mom.

"The more you see the problems of others," he said, "the smaller yours seem."

"So what do I do, Dad?"

"That's really simple: Love your wife. Do it seventeen seconds at a time, every single day, if that's what it takes."

I went home to my porch with a notebook and pen and listed as many simple acts of love as I could. Then I wrote down exactly what I needed to do to make them real. The last item took me a few weeks but I finally figured it out: *Help her rekindle her love for the written word.*

Once I started really *loving* Jade by doing simple things like being there when she got home, surprising her with Ben and Jerry's, taking her hand while walking down the mall, I realized that we weren't as far apart as I had feared. She just needed to be loved and I needed to remember how to do it.

I crossed the last item off my list the day I took her to Paper Gems.

"There's a cool new bookstore at the other end of the mall. You want to go?"

"I'm kind of tired. Is it worth the hike?"

"Oh, I think you will find it worthy of your time and effort."

"Lead on then, kind sir."

I took her hand—still one of my favorite feelings in the whole world—and walked with her past every other shop and restaurant on the downtown mall. We walked up to the door of the bookstore and I pulled on the handle.

"Hmmm. It's locked. It's too early for it to be closed."

"Good job, Mr. Conner." She smiled, knowing that the walk was worth it anyway because I would owe her something. "Now we get to hike all the way back without seeing so much as a paperback romance."

"You *live* a paperback romance, my dear. Anyway, I happen to have the key." I let go of her hand, reached into my pocket, and, without looking at her again, opened the door. I held it for her like a doorman, followed her in, and found the light switch.

"What is going on, Cole Conner?"

"Don't ask questions, just look around before we get caught. I hear the owner is a real piece of work."

She began to cry. "What have you done, Cole?"

"This is *your* store, Jade. I know it's not a child or a writing career. I can't give you either of those. But I can give you this because I love you. I love you . . . *and* I *love* you."

✤

FORTY-EIGHT

Suicide

THEY CAME IN SEPARATE CARS.

The next afternoon, Kendra arrived at 5:30 P.M. sharp in her mother's Audi.

Miles pulled in at 5:35 in his freshly waxed Saab.

Kendra hugged him when he got to the makeshift Reading Corner on the porch and he reciprocated awkwardly.

I took the moment. "I know things are a little strange right now, no use denying it, but for me it would mean a lot if you two tried out the love seat. Please? It's literally not had anyone in it yet and it's been sitting here nearly a week."

"Yeah," Kendra urged. "Come sit, Miles." She stepped to the love seat but Miles plopped into one of the chairs.

"No, thanks. Nothing personal."

Kendra tried so hard not to blush, she blushed. "Whatever." She sat in the chair across from him, crossed her legs, and leaned back.

"So, you two. Everything OK at home? Have a good night?"

They both shrugged in near-unison, their shoulders bouncing up and down like kids in a bad school choir.

"Wonderful. Well, you probably realize that this is supposed to be our last session. Tomorrow is Thanksgiving and I have never gone past it before." I gestured around the porch. "This is, I think it's safe to say, a special situation. Would you mind if we had one more meeting next Wednesday? I finally spoke to Travis and things are not so good at his place, so he can't join us for another session or two until his father leaves town again. He's supposed to leave this weekend."

"He's out?" asked Miles.

"Yes. And I'm impressed you remembered he was ever in. Well-done."

He looked back at me with shallow eyes. "I sorta remembered from class, but mostly 'cause everyone in the neighborhood where they used to live knew he was in jail. Didn't know he was back around, though."

Kendra remained quiet.

"So no. He's not comfortable coming today, but he said to tell you hello."

"Cool," Miles said.

Kendra nodded.

"Moving on. You have your pocket watches?"

Kendra pulled both from her purse and handed Miles's to me. I handed it around to him.

"Since we started, we've been talking about how it doesn't

take much time to make a major difference in someone's life. Seventeen seconds every day, right?"

"Yeah," Miles said, "but some of the things last more than that."

"They do, you are absolutely correct, and that's an astute observation. It's not the exact time that matters, though. Right, Kendra?"

"Uh-huh. Your dad just called them that because it was sort of an average. And because that's how long they thought it took for Flick to die." Kendra looked at me with an apology in her tired eyes.

"It's all right to talk about. You're also correct. The things my father did for people, the things he taught me to do for people, sometimes they took five seconds, like opening a door, sometimes they took an hour, like changing a tire for someone or giving them a ride."

Just as I began to pivot the conversation, I heard the front door open behind me. "Mrs. Conner!" Kendra jumped up and turned toward her.

Jade met her with arms wide open.

While they giggled and whispered, I rolled my eyes at Miles. "Girls, right?"

"Yeah."

"You OK over there, Miles?"

"I guess."

"Your coach all right with you being here?"

"I don't know. Probably not."

Suddenly I found myself scouring the street, even as Miles continued talking.

"He might be mad, but I had to come. I missed last time."

Kendra had followed Jade off the porch and over to her Vespa. They were obviously sharing a funny story. My focus went from the road back to the girls and back to Miles. "You heard us in the gym, didn't you?"

Miles had taken an instant interest in his iPhone.

"Miles?"

"It's all good."

Kendra was back and Jade was beeping her toy horn on her Vespa and heading off to Paper Gems.

"Sorry," she said, retaking her seat.

Everything about her looked brighter and healthier. *The Jade effect.*

"Better?" I asked her.

"Much."

Finally time to pivot. "This week, I'm going to tell you a story that I've pieced together from Mom's and Dad's journals along with some amateur investigative reporting."

"Cool," Miles said.

"Perhaps. You can decide after you hear it . . . It happened when my dad was still working as an accountant. He hadn't yet tried his hand at radio and realized how much he loved it. One day, he was walking to the garage where he'd had his oil changed. He'd left the car in the morning and decided he had time to walk back to pick it up after work. Get some exercise. Enjoy the weather. But he got about halfway there and realized he wouldn't make it on time. Before he could even consider sticking his thumb out, someone stopped and offered him a ride. As chance—or karma—would have it, it was an old friend from high school, a lifeguard at Chris Greene Lake the summer of 1970. They hadn't seen each other in at least five years, Dad said."

"That dude did your dad a Seventeen Second Miracle then. Gave him a ride to the shop."

"Correct. They made it in time, just as the cashier was closing out for the day. The mechanics themselves were long gone. Dad paid for the car and as soon as he got outside, the cashier walked out the front door with the shop's night deposit bank bag and locked it behind her. The bays were shut, the lights were off. Just like that, Dad was alone in the parking lot and crumpling up the paper mats the shop used to keep the floorboards clean."

"I always chuck those, too," Miles said.

"Dad saw a Dumpster in the corner of the lot and he got back out of the car to throw the trash away. When he got to the trash bin, he noticed a young man walking into the tree line with a backpack on. He called to him.

"*Hello?* But the boy kept walking.

"*Hello, son, everything all right?* Dad asked him. Finally the boy stopped and looked at him. Dad said he didn't look sad, or scared, or intimidated. Just lost.

"*Are you all right?* Dad asked again.

"The boy quickly made up a story about cutting through the trees to get home, in spite of the obvious. It was an industrial area. On the other side of the tree line, maybe thirty yards deep is all, was a ratty industrial park and some train tracks."

"He was shoplifting, wasn't he?" asked Kendra.

"Not at all. My father convinced the boy to come back out of the trees to the parking lot. He said he was worried about him going that way and that dark would cover them too soon anyway. The boy, and I keep calling him a boy but Dad said he was more like a young teenager, maybe thirteen or fourteen, he came out and sat on the steps of the shop. He wouldn't take a ride home from Dad, but he obviously enjoyed the conversation. They talked for almost an hour until the boy agreed to let Dad call his home from a phone booth in the parking lot. The boy's father came. Guess who it was?"

"The shop owner," guessed Miles.

"One of your dad's tax customers?" Kendra tried.

"It was Dad's pal from high school. The man who'd given him a ride and dropped him off at the shop just an hour earlier."

"Wow," Miles said.

"There's more."

Miles and Kendra were both on the edges of their patio chairs.

"The next morning the boy's father called my dad to thank him again for interceding with his son. He wept on the phone and said it saved his son's life."

"How?" they both asked, now in better concert.

"Dad's friend found something in his son's backpack that morning."

"Drugs," Kendra said, matter-of-factly.

"No."

"Beer?" Miles took a turn.

I looked at them both and ended the story as simply as I could, as simply as Dad had told me: "A gun."

Miles spoke first. "That's . . . Wow . . . Dude. Your dad pretty much saved that kid."

"If he did," I said, "then he saved more than *one* life. The young man went on to graduate from AHS, marry a girl he met at Virginia Tech, and raise a very large family. I think he has six kids now. He followed in his father's footsteps and chose a career in education."

Recognition sparkled in Kendra's eyes. I continued, "A few years ago, he took over from his father as the principal of Albemarle High School."

"O. M. G." Miles took a full second to say each letter.

"That was it then," Kendra said. "That was the Seventeen Second Miracle that made up for Flick drowning."

"No," Miles answered, as I would have. "It's not a trade-off, right, Mr. C.? It's not like Mr. Buhl makes up for Flick."

"But if it hadn't been for Flick," Kendra said, "maybe he wouldn't have started his daily Seventeen Second Miracles. And if he hadn't started them, he might not have stopped to help Mr. Buhl. And if your dad hadn't stopped, our principal might not exist today. Neither would Mrs. Buhl or—oh my gosh—the twins. They're freshmen this year. So it's almost like Flick died for them, and she didn't even know it."

They both looked at me as if I sat as some referee waiting to pick a winner. I pointed at each of them. "Brilliant."

FORTY-NINE

Speed

"CAN YOU COME OVER TO MY HOUSE? *PLEASE?*"

Kendra's voice was quiet on the other end of the phone.

"Why?"

"Dad and Miles are having a fight in his study."

"And?"

"It's about you."

"Who?" I switched the phone from one ear to the other.

"You. Basketball. Me. College. Could you *please* come?"

"This really isn't my business—"

"Please?"

I pulled the phone away and rapped the mouthpiece against my forehead.

"I'll bring Jade."

"Thank you, thank you. Please speed."

"Text me the address."

"Thank you, thank you."

Jade was reading a book on the couch.

"I need you," I said.

She shut her book and made a tigress noise and matching hand gesture.

"Not like that. Miles is in trouble."

I relayed the phone call as we ran to the car and sped toward Kendra's house.

We approached her driveway and noticed immediately that Miles's car was already gone.

We got out of the BMW and walked to the door. I looked at Jade and mouthed, *Thank you.* Then I looked at my watch. 9:15 P.M. *I should not be ringing Coach Max's doorbell at 9:15.*

Kendra opened the ornate front door precisely as I pushed the doorbell. Her cheeks were wet and her eyes filled with something between fear and disdain. "He raced off."

"What happened?" I asked, and Jade reached inside to take Kendra's hand.

Kendra wiped an eye and smudged mascara beneath.

Jade sweetly cleaned it off with her thumb.

The garage opened and a deep voice echoed across the concrete. "Go," it said.

I stepped off and met Coach Max at the driveway. The floodlight on the garage cast a giant Max shadow.

He was pointing at my car. "Go."

"I am so sorry about all this. Kendra just thought I could help. She didn't mean to upset you."

The veins in Coach Max's neck were bulging. "Do you know what basketball could do for Miles?"

I didn't have time to even consider an answer, save actually *give* one.

"Full scholarship. Playing time as a freshman, maybe. Pro ball someday. Maybe here. Maybe in Europe. And a state championship as a senior. Do you know how many people get state championships as seniors? Do you know when AHS has had one? Do you know what that means?" The words came out in short, white puffs. "No, you don't."

He'd said so much I didn't know what *that* was anymore.

"Who gave you the right, anyway? Who gave you permission to meet with Miles for your psychobabble lessons? And right when the season starts, no less."

"And Kendra, too? Right?"

"You didn't answer me."

"No one did, technically, but you know the Discussions are not school required. They're not even associated with the school except that Principal Buhl helps recommend kids."

"And what's so special about these two that they needed your little class?"

You tell me, I thought. "They are both remarkable people, Coach Max. You must know that, right? You must know how special your daughter is? How talented she is? How gifted she is on the basketball court?"

"Sidelines," he corrected with force. "Just go. I want Kendra inside right now, *right now*, and Miles at practice tomorrow."

As I watched him do an about-face and march into his garage, I wondered what my father would have done.

Kendra hugged Jade and me and slinked into her home.

I stood my ground and Coach Max stared me down like a schoolyard bully. "I'll make you a deal, Coach."

He didn't answer, but he also didn't hit me, so I continued on. "Play a game of one-on-one with your daughter tonight. If you win, she's done with the Discussions. So is Miles. But if she wins, they both attend as long and as often as they want."

He shifted his attention to the sand-filled portable basketball hoop in the driveway, then looked back at me.

I took a step toward him with my hand extended.

After another dramatic stare-down he took three steps in my direction, shook my hand, and pointed to my car.

I think I breathed again when Jade backed us out of the driveway and sped off.

We checked every street in the neighborhood before heading back into town.

We went north on 29 to Fashion Square Mall and circled the parking lot looking for Miles's car.

We cruised by the bowling ally and three movie theaters before thinking to also check our own house on Jefferson Park Avenue. As we passed Wayside Chicken, I bet Jade a diamond necklace he'd be parked in the driveway and sitting on the porch.

He wasn't.

Jade let me off the hook.

FIFTY

Guilt

IS THAT MY PHONE?

I was half asleep, or slightly more, when a buzzing on our nightstand startled me.

"Phoooone," Jade grumbled from under the blanket.

I stretched for it and flipped it open with one hand, wondering who would be calling us so early on Thanksgiving Day. "Hello?"

"Mr. Conner?"

"Mmm-hmmm." I squinted my eyes and tried to read the time on the alarm clock.

"Can you come to the station this morning?"

I pushed myself up. "Of course." I cleared my throat. "It's over? You have someone?"

"We're set when you are. See you as soon as possible." The voice hung up and I realized I didn't have any idea who I'd spoken to.

I looked at the clock again: 7:15. "Jade." I shook her shoulder. "Get up."

She did and I relayed all I knew.

In less than twenty minutes, we'd both showered and dressed. Jade towel-dried her hair while I sloshed mouthwash.

She asked me questions at two thousand miles per hour that I did not know the answers to.

I drove us to police headquarters on Market Street, where we were met by the fire captain in the lobby, the same man who'd given us the news that the fire wasn't the accident we'd prayed it was. This time he wore a uniform and badge instead of his thick yellow firefighting garb.

A Charlottesville police officer asked us to empty our pockets, walk through airport-like security, and sign-in. The station was almost empty and I wondered if we were the only reason they weren't home getting ready for turkey and football.

The captain led us to an elevator. "We just picked up a suspect."

Jade looked at me as if *I'd* said it.

"Last night one of CPD's detectives was reviewing the 911 log and made a connection."

I wondered what kind of strength it took for him not to say, *I told you so.* But after nearly two weeks in limbo and a roller coaster of strain with Jade and the uncertainty she'd ever feel safe again, I wouldn't have cared if he'd said it right out loud and right to my face.

"Thank goodness," said Jade, who then put both arms around one of mine and squeezed. "It's over." She put her forehead against my arm and took a long, comforting breath before exhaling and squeezing me one more time in relief.

"So who?" I asked.

The elevator door opened and he gestured for Jade to enter.

We followed to the third floor and the elevator opened to a sea of empty cubicles and glass-walled meeting rooms.

At the end of a long hallway along the left side of the open floor, we saw the backs of two officers, two other suits, and a woman in a corner conference room.

The captain led us in and we saw one person.

A young man seated with his back to the door.

He was in a wheelchair.

My mouth fell open.

Jade covered hers.

"Mr. and Mrs. Conner, you know Travis, I believe."

I still couldn't speak.

Jade walked around the corner of the table and tried to look him in the eye.

He avoided her.

Like a whip, she raised her hand from her hip and slapped him across the face.

One of the officers pulled her back from behind with both arms.

"How could you do this?" Jade's voice rose to a shrill squeak. "I let you into my life!"

The officer continued to restrain her.

Mrs. Nielson watched the scene with her arms folded across her chest and her eyes glazed and steady.

"Is this true, Travis?" I moved to face him.

He nodded once.

"I want to hear it." I looked at the captain; he looked at the suits.

"Go ahead, Mr. Nielson," one of them said. "Tell Mr. Conner what you told us."

Travis looked at his mother. Then Jade. Then me.

He said it just the way he'd probably been rehearsing for days.

"I started the fire."

FIFTY-ONE

Doubts

"I DON'T BELIEVE HIM."

There are only so many ways to say the words.

I told Travis's mother, the investigators, the captain, Jade, and later, Kendra.

"I don't believe him."

I said that even though everything pointed the other way. The reason the fire department got there so fast was because the first 911 call came in *before* the fire started. There were six calls total, and all but *one* were made within two minutes of one another. The first was made sixteen minutes before the others. It was made from Travis's cell phone.

The juvenile crimes prosecutor agreed to argue for probation before the judge. Given Travis's record—he had none—and unique family situation, he was moderately confident the judge would be lenient. He also offered to tell the judge, who was in chambers, that the confession was questionable.

"But confessions are confessions," he said to us.

With Jade behind me shooting daggers from her eyes, I told the prosecutor that I would not press charges or otherwise cooperate in the investigation until I was convinced we knew the whole story.

Shortly after 3:00 P.M., Travis was released to his mother's custody and a hearing was scheduled for Monday morning.

On our way home, I argued again that Travis could not have done it. I didn't know why he would take the blame but I knew he was innocent.

"He was there, Cole. He called in the fire."

"That's just another thing that doesn't fit. Why would he call 911 and then set a fire? How did he get there in the first place? How do we even know he was the one who used the phone? He didn't do it."

Just to humor me, Jade quizzed me a final time on my clients, who I might have upset, whose portfolio I might have shrunk, etc.

She also asked me again about my former students, the fifty-plus young men and women who'd been a part of the Discussions for the past ten years.

"It's just not possible," I said.

"Cole, *everyone* has enemies."

"I dispute that, but even *if* true, not everyone has enemies willing to set your business on fire. Perhaps they avoid you at the store, or toss your mail when it's delivered to the wrong box instead of bringing it over, but they don't burn your store down. Besides, who's to say it wasn't one of *your* many enemies. Somebody bought a book with the last page missing."

She didn't find it funny.

We agreed to assume Travis's confession was legitimate, though we couldn't look at each other when we did.

Kendra sent me a text message that night asking if she could come by.

I told her I thought it wasn't smart without her father's permission.

So Kendra sent a text message to Jade, who grinned like a prisoner for having given Jade her cell phone number.

JADE: sorry hun . . . not yet
KENDRA: yes! Dad says its ok
JADE: really??
KENDRA: yes!
JADE: did you win?
KENDRA: :)
JADE: tomorrow!

I fired up the patio heaters and Jade and I had dinner on our porch for the first time since Labor Day. After we cleared the dishes, we went back out to the porch.

Jade walked to the love seat and began to sit, but at the last moment stopped herself and looked down at it as if it were occupied. She didn't say a word; she dragged the two chairs from the table to the edge of the porch closest to the heater, and sat down. She patted the armrest of the other chair.

In marriages of all kinds, the good ones, the broken ones,

and the ones that need everything from Band-Aids to careful fine-tuning, there are conversations we never forget.

The quiet moments at the end of endless days when kids are asleep, at college, or home with their own children.

The post-tension, post-fight, post-regretful discussions that start with *I'm sorry* and end with *I love you.*

Under the stars with cars and pedestrians passing by, Jade thanked me for the time I'd devoted to the Discussions for so long, and for the good I'd done.

I told her what I'd long felt, but never expressed—at least not well. She'd stayed with me when others wouldn't have during the early years when I was more married to the past than I was to her. Without knowing it, she'd brought me the same balance my mother had brought my father.

I also told her I loved her more than the legacy, more than the stories, more than the memories of my father. "I love my mother, I love my father, but *you're* my life now. In a thousand years, yours is the hand I'll reach for when we get lost in a crowd in heaven."

Jade lifted her legs up onto the chair, heels on the edge, and hugged her knees. She told me how blessed we'd been with the Discussions to have so many children in our lives over so many years. "You and God know I wanted kids, but we've had the next-best thing. Kids that come, drink a little soda, eat some snacks, listen to our lectures, and then go home."

"Think of the money we've saved on food alone," I said.

"And college."

Later we stared at each other in bed, waiting for the other's eyes to close first, our heads so close I was more on her pillow than mine. But sleep didn't come easy for either one of us.

Jade worried about just how safe she really was.

I worried about Travis.

But for the night, we were home.

FIFTY-TWO

Decision

IT WENT AS SUSPECTED.

I received a call Monday morning from the prosecutor saying that the judge refused to throw out the confession. Instead, he sentenced Travis to two years' probation and ordered 240 hours' community service. It would, in essence, be a part-time job.

Also, without us knowing or making a request, a restraining order was issued preventing him from coming within fifty feet of the store or our house.

The prosecutor told us he was pleased because it was a fair measure of justice, even though he and everyone else remained doubtful that Travis had snuck out of his home after his midnight curfew, found a ride downtown, called 911, started the fire—thought to have been ignited with gasoline, a rag, and a match tossed in a broken window—and returned home unseen and completely undetected. He also joined us in wondering who, if not Travis, had made the call and why he'd taken the blame.

He also told us it could have been much, much worse and that if Travis had no trouble during probation, the matter would be expunged from his record.

That afternoon I sent Travis a text telling him he was welcome in our home anytime and that the restraining order would be enforced only if we wanted it to be, and we didn't want it to be. I pled with him to come to our next Discussion, even if he were to be the only one. I was beginning to wonder if the Discussions were, by default, over for the year.

When Wednesday arrived, I nearly broke into song when Kendra arrived in her mother's silver Audi with Miles riding shotgun.

I embraced Kendra first. "I cannot tell you how happy I am to see you here."

Kendra put her arm around Miles. "Have you met my best friend, Miles?"

I hugged him, too. "Yes, I have."

Miles pulled away and looked me in the eye. "I'm sorry about the other night, Mr. C. I . . . I . . . I just wanted to make a statement, you know. Stand up for myself. I didn't mean for Coach to get on your case."

"I know, Miles."

Kendra added, "I'm the one who called them, Miles. It's my fault, too."

"No harm, no foul." I winked at Miles.

He looked back at the grass. "So I'm off the basketball team.

First, Coach threatened to bench me. He said my attitude would drag the team down. Then I told him he could do whatever he wanted. So he kicked me off."

"Oh, Miles, I'm sorry. I know this was a big year for you."

He shrugged and kept his focus downward.

"You know what, Miles? Not to worry, with a letter from me and great grades, and maybe some other recommendations I can help you with, we'll get you what you deserve."

"I think I already have," he said. I couldn't be sure because his head was still down, but it sure looked like he was fighting a smile.

"You all right?"

"Yeah, and honestly, Mr. C., I'm kinda looking forward to watching from the bleachers and doing some cheering of my own for once. Maybe even at some girls' games."

"We'll see," Kendra said with a grin.

I invited them to christen the love seat, at last, but Kendra sat in a chair instead and said, "We better not. Not yet. We might end up there again, right, Miles? But for now, we're going to figure out who we are alone before we figure out what we are together."

"She's right," Miles said. "Plus we were thinking maybe you and Mrs. Conner could be the first."

"Fair enough," I said.

Miles looked eager to move on. "Is Trav coming?"

I hesitated, knowing they were going to find out eventually. But not today. Not from me. "I don't think so. His father is still in town, uh, visiting, I guess, and I suspect they're spending some family time together. They've been through a lot."

They both nodded in agreement.

"It looks like we will have to wrap up the Discussions without Travis," I said.

"That's not right. We can't go on without him, right? He's part of our group. Can't we just wait for the last meeting until he can be here?"

My heart melted, then sank. "We'll see. But for today, I think it's time for an assignment. Something to take away right now and do, then report back right away. What do you say? Something different?"

"I'm in."

"Me too."

"Wonderful. I want you to get out of here and go perform a Seventeen Second Miracle. I don't care if it takes five seconds or five minutes. You know the drill. And I'm not going to tell you what to do or how to do it. This is up to you—*completely.* Go surprise someone with something nice, something unexpected. Put a smile on their face and give them something to write in their journals. Think of it. Tonight someone might just pull out a ragged old notebook and write: *The nicest girl stopped today and helped me weed my flower bed, or carry in my groceries.* Or maybe, *A handsome young man read to me today at the nursing home. I don't remember his name, but his face shined.*

"Right now?" Kendra asked.

"Indeed. Right now. Come back in thirty minutes or less. Just like Domino's."

It was the first time all month, with the exception of my failed experiment with Travis, that Miles looked engaged and excited with something other than Kendra's legs or his treasured iPhone.

They stopped at the car and debated for a moment whether to go on foot or drive. After just a few seconds they passed the car and proceeded down the sidewalk. They walked like friends, a comfortable distance apart, gabbing and pointing and enjoying the company.

I ran back inside, called Jade to check in and let her know two of the three had arrived, and fetched another of my father's journals. When I returned back outside, Kendra and Miles were standing in front of the house.

"So soon?" I asked while joining them in the yard.

"We had an idea." Kendra looked at Miles.

"Yeah," he said. "We thought maybe we could go to Travis's house. That could be our miracle for today."

I arrived at their side. "I don't know. I'd hate to interrupt their family time."

Kendra looked at Miles again for support. "Mr. C., Miles and I were saying we sort of miss Travis. We thought we'd surprise him, right? It's been a while. We haven't seen him since the fire."

"Actually," Miles added confidently, "we haven't seen him since the . . . you know . . ."

All three of us knew what he was going to say next.

"I don't know. I think his mother is sensitive about their living arrangements. You understand."

"If we don't care, why should she?"

Another reminder that through the years, my students have taught me as much as—*or more than*—I've taught them.

"You really want to pay a quick, quick visit?"

Nods.

"All right, hop in." I gestured toward my BMW and went inside to get my keys and wallet. Out of the corner of my eye, I saw Kendra do what looked like some kind of cheerleader sidekick.

On the drive over I had Kendra try calling Beth from my cell phone.

"No answer."

"Try texting her."

Unresponsive.

"Do either of you have Travis's phone number?" I asked. My mind was racing, trying to decide whether I should tell them about the confession, let Travis do it, or hope it wouldn't come up.

Kendra and Miles both admitted embarrassment at not knowing his number. I thought how ironic it was that I had been thinking about Travis and his phone all night but didn't know its number.

They made idle chatter as we drove into Albemarle County and toward Miles and Travis's neighborhood at the farthest stretches of the school district.

Miles shared rumors about Travis's abusive dad and the crazy speculation about what he'd done to land in prison in the first place. "I hear it's not his first time," Miles said.

"We hope for the best," I said. "Everyone deserves a fresh start."

I pulled into the neighborhood and weaved my way toward Travis's house on the southernmost street before the roads became gravel dead ends. A block before his house, I pulled over and put the car in park.

"Is this it?" Kendra was looking back and forth between the two houses closest to us.

"No. We're still a block away. Look, guys, I need to tell you something. You make your own judgments, but I want you to know that I have faith in Travis."

"What are you talking about, Mr. C.?"

"Miles, you and Kendra should know that Travis confessed to setting the fire at Paper Gems."

"No way. *No way* he did that." Miles shook his head.

"Did he say why?" Kendra had unbuckled her seat belt and was leaning over the seat.

"No. I didn't ask why because I don't believe he did it." I paused. "Do you still want to visit him?"

"Now more than ever," Miles answered for both of them.

Travis was out in front of his house when we pulled up. I had never seen him look so trapped in his chair before. When Miles got out of the car and walked toward him, Travis looked like he wanted to disappear. He even rolled backward a couple of feet before dropping his shoulders and looking at the ground. Miles walked right up to Travis, knelt on the ground in front of him, and put his hands on his shoulders.

Without looking up, Travis said, "I'm sorry."

"What for, Trav?"

"For torching the store."

"Look at me, man."

Travis looked up.

Miles said, "No matter what happened, I believe in you, Travis. I don't believe you would do anything to hurt the Conners or me or Kendra. So no matter what, I believe in you."

The whole exchange only took long enough for me, Kendra, and Mrs. Nielson to gather around the pair. Not more than seventeen seconds.

FIFTY-THREE

Answers

MOM: Turn on TV
ME: OK

I hurried into the kitchen and turned on the little set hanging under the counter. I braced myself with both hands as I saw a local correspondent standing in front of Travis Nielson's house. Behind the reporter were a few policemen, some neighbors, and yards of yellow tape.

"Jade!"

She joined me as the woman on WVIR news was saying, "As I said, details are sketchy right now. The police haven't made an official statement but neighbors say they heard gunshots at around 9:00 P.M. The police and rescue squad arrived on the scene ten or fifteen minutes later. Just before we got here, one or two bodies—again, we don't have all the details, yet—one or two bodies in body bags were removed from the house behind me and one person was taken away by police. We'll know more when we get an official statement. Recapping, what appears to be a homicide has rocked a quiet community in Albemarle County. One or two people are believed dead and the apparent . . . apparently the alleged shooter is in custody. Back to you, Dave."

I wasn't sure whether to make a call or say a prayer. I'm not sure I had enough breath to do either.

I also wasn't sure whether to go to the hospital, the morgue, or the police station. So we decided it would be best to wait until we knew more. We moved into the living room and turned on the bigger TV, as if a larger screen would reveal more of the stunning story. We forced ourselves to sit, both admitting it was maddening to watch normal Monday night television, which we almost never did, while waiting for news that could only be bad, terrible, or horrific.

Mom called, and while she was on the phone with Jade, Kendra called my cell. She had already been talking to Miles, who was already headed to her house. We tried to convince each other that we shouldn't assume anything. We would know soon enough.

At 10:30, the station skipped a commercial and put up the breaking news banner. "There was a fatal shooting tonight in Albemarle County. Join us at eleven o'clock for coverage by the Channel 29 news team."

I took out my phone to call the police station and it rang before I could look up the number.

"Cole Conner."

"Mr. Conner, could you come down to the station? The precinct on the east side of town?"

"Of course. What's this about?"

I could tell the police officer put his hand over the mouthpiece and passed my question along to someone else. "No, sir, I can't. Please come down and we will clear everything up for you."

Jade was already putting her coat on when I slipped the phone back into my pocket. I wanted to suggest that she stay home in case it was really bad news, but I knew I would be wasting my time.

The only words said between our house and the police station were Jade's. "I don't care whether he started the fire or not. I pray he's OK."

I parked in an employees' only spot in front of the building and started to jog to the doors. Then I stopped, turned around, and waited for Jade to catch up. I reached out for her hand. She took off her glove, intertwined her fingers with mine, and we walked in side by side.

"We're the Conners. Somebody just called and asked us to come down."

"Come in through the door to your right." The door buzzed and opened into what was a now-familiar routine of searches and metal detectors. A kind-looking woman in a slightly too-small uniform led us to an interview room. Inside was a conference table that looked like it could have been bought on sale at Office Depot. Sitting in plastic chairs were Mrs. Nielson, a woman in a smart business outfit, a man who could not have been anything else but a lawyer, and two policemen. Travis's mother looked serious but her eyes were dry.

"You are Mr. and Mrs. Cole Conner, correct?"

"Yes, sir."

"I'm Jeff Martindale, with the city prosecutor's office, this is Adrienne Jonas, with Social Services."

"Pleased to meet you both." I wanted them to tell us Travis was OK. Every word they said in the meantime made me want to crawl out of my skin and out the door.

"You know Mrs. Nielson here." He didn't wait for an answer. "She was arrested earlier this evening for the murder of her husband. She has agreed to cooperate with us fully on two conditions, the first of which is that we bring you here."

"What's going on, Beth?" I tried to sound calm.

Her face relaxed and she took a breath. "Travis's father came over to the house. He and Travis got in a terrible argument. Bill started hitting Travis with an extension cord. I tried to stop him. But . . . but he hit me in the face." She instinctively reached up and touched the beginnings of a bruise on the side of her jaw. "I got the gun out of the desk drawer and shot him." She turned to the attorney. "Now, the rest of our deal."

"Mr. Conner," he began, "Mrs. Nielson is going to be held pending trial. We may strike a deal, we may not. But she's asked if Travis could be placed in your custody in the meantime."

I looked at Jade but she answered for us both before I could even made eye contact with her.

"Yes."

"Depending on the outcome," he continued, "it could be

until his eighteenth birthday, and we wouldn't want to move him twice. He needs a long-term option."

It still doesn't surprise me how lightning-quick we answered, in crisp, instinctive unison, like a duet that's never sung with anyone else: "Of course."

"Are you sure?" the social worker said. "Do you want to think about it overnight? For a few nights, perhaps?"

Again, as one: "We're sure."

"All right," she said and grinned at the attorney.

Had she won a bet? I thought.

"Travis is going to spend the night with us," she continued. "Come downtown to the county office building tomorrow morning after nine o'clock. Ask for me and we'll do all the paperwork. Then, unless there is a hitch overnight, you can take Travis home."

"Thank you." Jade got up, shook everyone's hand, and with a you'd-better-not-touch-me look, walked to where Beth sat and gave her a hug. "Thank you. Thank you for trusting us. We'll take good care of him. I promise."

"I'm counting on it." She talked to Jade, but looked at me.

FIFTY-FOUR

Coming Home

"I WANT TO SEE MILES."

It was the first thing Travis said after we got him in the car and his wheelchair in the trunk. That was, in fact, the first and only thing he said until we arrived at Kendra's house.

Coach Max opened the door and waved us in. He looked less intimidating than he had a few nights earlier, but his body language told me we would never be hoops buddies.

Kendra ran to give us each a hug.

Travis rolled right past her and over to Miles, who looked small in an oversized recliner.

"What you said at my house. Did you really mean it?"

"Yeah. I really meant it. I got your back."

"I didn't do it. I didn't torch the store."

I walked over and put my arms on his shoulders. "We knew you couldn't do anything like that, Travis. Will you tell us what really happened?"

"Last night wasn't the first time my dad came to pick a fight. The night of the fire, he came over to get some money from Mom. She didn't have any and they argued, just like the billion times before. I yelled at him and told him to get out." Travis looked up at Miles. "Then he cussed and asked me where I got my attitude from. Why I was standing up to him all of a sudden. I told him that I was meeting with you guys at Paper Gems and that you helped me believe that I can still do good even though I couldn't save Trista."

Miles edged forward to the front of the recliner.

"He told me that I would never be no good and that he wished it had been me under that car instead of my sister. I told him I didn't care what he thought anymore and that he could go to hell." Travis took a long breath and looked at me this time.

Though I tried to mask it, I felt a rush of pride. I'll probably never know whether Travis saw it or not.

"That's when my dad left. But before he did, he got right in my face and whispered, 'Gem Bookstores. That's the bookstore that used to be downtown, isn't it?'

"I knew from the look on his face what he was gonna do. He was in jail for some kind of insurance thing. Fraud, I guess. I think arson was like his hobby. So I went in my room so Mom couldn't hear and called 911 and said there was a fire at Paper Gems. I figured the cops would show up right when he did. Either they would catch him or he would see them and chicken out." Travis looked down and his tone softened. "I didn't think he would get there so fast. I'm really sorry about that part."

"And once you heard about the fire," I said, "you were afraid your dad would come after you and your mom if you turned him in, so you just took the blame."

"Yeah. I was scared for Mom. Turns out she pretty much takes care of herself."

"Yes, she does," I said. "She surely does. Now, who's ready for a Discussion?"

Travis rode with me in the BMW. I placed him up front and stored his wheelchair in the backseat next to Jade. Miles and Kendra got a head start, because even with Travis's help it took me a few minutes to solve the wheelchair-through-the-door puzzle.

He even poked fun at me when I pinched my thumb between the chair and the doorjamb.

Teasing never felt so good.

As we neared town, Travis began punching buttons on the complicated dash.

I grinned my approval and he fidgeted with the elaborate stereo until hearing my mother's voice on WCHV. She was, it seemed, finishing a phone interview with the afternoon host. "Thanks for the time, Blake, I appreciate it so very much. And I hope if there's anyone listening that can help, that they won't hesitate. Not for a second. It could mean the world. This is your chance," she concluded, "to perform a Seventeen Second Miracle today."

Blake thanked her for calling in and turned it over to the news desk.

I tried calling my mother but got voice mail. I called the station, too, and when I asked for Blake was dumped into a contest line that rang and rang. So I tried again, curious for details, and got Blake's voice mail: "DJB, leave a message."

"What was that about?" Jade asked from the backseat.

"I wish I knew."

I turned to look at Travis, but he'd swiveled his head and attention out the window to the houses that became closer and closer together as we approached the city.

We arrived downtown and were surprised that each of the usual guaranteed-to-be-free spots were taken. We settled on a paid lot two blocks away. The sidewalks were filled with more Christmas shoppers than usual. The pedestrian mall looked like an anthill. There were dozens of people coming and going, but nobody standing still. My palms grew sweaty and my heartbeat quickened when I saw that the center of the ant activity was Paper Gems.

We wove through the throng and somebody called my mother's name.

The crowd parted.

She and Candace appeared in front of us. She waved us toward the store and the commotion inside.

"What is this?" I asked.

"Look."

There were people lined up at the cash register and out the door. Each person held at least one book. Many had several stacked in their arms.

"These are the people who've attended the Discussions, or whose lives have been affected by the miracles."

"All of them?"

"All of them."

Something wasn't right and Jade was the first to realize it. She began to cry and pulled Candace into her arms. Then she stuck one arm out and snagged my mom.

People weren't in line to *buy* soggy books; they were *donating* books.

"Some people are donating books from their personal collections," Candace said. "Others bought them from other stores. So far we have accepted more than nine hundred books."

Among the crowd I saw Miles and Kendra sitting on a bench marveling at the miracle.

Miles saw me and came to shake my hand. "Where's Travis?"

I nodded toward the corner, where Travis was hidden behind a wall of people.

Miles worked his way through the crowd and began pushing the wheelchair. A path cleared between the front of the store and the Reading Corner. They found Kendra sitting on one side of the love seat someone brought from the porch. She wore a smile bright enough to warm even the coldest of grieving winter hearts.

Miles stopped the chair in front of the love seat and locked the wheels. Then he turned around with his back to the chair and motioned for Travis to climb on. Miles turned around and placed him in the middle of the seat and sat next to him.

Had there ever been more love in one seat? I thought.

In the crowd I saw radio station employees, old clients of Dad's, old and new clients of mine. Students who'd been to my Discussions and their friends who hadn't but whose lives had been touched. Parents, teachers, neighbors, even Coach Max, who gave me a handshake and a biography of Larry Bird.

"She creamed me," he said.

I smiled. "I'm sorry."

"Don't be. I'm sure not. We played until midnight. We've been playing ever since. I haven't seen her smile that much since her mom left. She even let me read some stuff in a journal she's been keeping. I . . . I don't really know her like I thought."

"Do you know how special she is?"

"I do."

"That's a good start." I lifted my arms to hug him and he simply shook my hand again.

"Slow your roll, buddy." He slapped me on the back and stepped away with a smile as big as Kendra's. "Easy now."

Mom gathered me up, and she and Jade looped an arm through mine and walked me through the mass.

Full hugs, half-hugs, more handshakes, and more *Thank-yous* than anyone deserves in a lifetime.

Mom stepped up to the front door and pulled me alongside her. "Do you have your pocket watch, Son?"

I pulled it from my pocket.

She took it from me and held it up. Dozens of others followed, holding their watches high in the air for everyone to see.

Miles, Kendra, and Travis all held theirs up as well.

"We are all graduates today, Son. And your father is so proud of you."

I didn't know how to reply, what to say next. So I whispered simply, "No words. I just . . . I just don't know . . ."

FIFTY-FIVE

The Final

OUR LAST DISCUSSION TOOK PLACE YESTERDAY, THE FOURTH OF December.

Jade, Travis, Miles, Kendra, and I left early from the store. We drove the BMW, a temporary solution since Travis preferred to travel in his wheelchair but wasn't yet ready to ride in his mother's van with its colorful flames. We weren't sure he ever would, and if it meant keeping him in our lives, we were prepared to buy a custom-fit van ourselves.

"Where are we going?" Kendra asked.

"You'll see."

"How far is it?"

"Just ride."

"Are we seeing someone?"

"Kendra!" yelled our car choir.

She laughed, and we tried not to laugh, too, but we did anyway.

We drove first to Chris Greene Lake and each of us tossed a white carnation in the water in memory of Flick.

"Mr. Conner," Kendra said, her eyes fixed firmly on the carnation as it drifted away from the shore. "Have you ever wondered what the biggest Seventeen Second Miracle ever was?"

"I'm not sure, Kendra. There have been so many miracles performed by so many people on so many days."

"Well, I know," she said. "The most amazing Seventeen Second Miracle ever was that Sparks forgave your dad. It just *has* to be that."

My eyes found the carnation I'd tossed in the water drifting toward the stem of another. "That's a lovely thought, Kendra. Forgiving those we love is always a miracle, no matter how long it takes."

Next we drove next to a cemetery none of them knew.

"Is this your dad's?" Kendra asked and I winked at her in the rearview mirror.

We parked at the base of a hill and I helped Travis into his chair. I pushed him through the freshly cut grass while the others followed Jade to a grave at the top.

There in the mid-morning sunlight stood my mother. She met each with open arms and a flower.

Travis and I were the last to arrive at the marker: LISA ANN EVANS, SEPTEMBER 4, 1962–SEPTEMBER 4, 1970.

"This is Flick. Your sister," Miles said and my mother nodded.

I waited for the quiet to settle and pass.

"Are you ready for your final exam?" I asked.

"We are," Travis answered for all three.

"Then take out those watches."

They did and I smiled when I saw Mom and Jade pull out watches of their own.

"You have seventeen seconds to tell me why *you* think you were selected by Principal Buhl to become part of the Seventeen Second Miracle fraternity."

1—2—3—4—5—6—7—8—9—10—11—12—13—14—15—16—17.

Miles: "To learn there are other worlds besides mine. To follow my own dreams and to be brave enough to be myself."

Travis: "That I'm not a lost cause and that the miracles go both ways. And, I guess, to not feel so dang sorry for myself."

Kendra: "To be *me* more often."

"Interesting," I said. "Go on."

"It feels weird to say, Mr. Conner, but I just think maybe I need to perform some Seventeen Second Miracles for myself every now and then."

"If I were giving grades, you just scored a 4.0."

She beamed.

"Kendra, I will always be grateful for you. You did more for us during these weeks together than you'll ever know. You were our glue, our compass, our rock, and our watch. Our time together would not have been nearly as valuable without you. You were part of *our* miracle. And look what else you got: a best friend." I nodded toward Miles.

She threw her arms around me. "Thank you for everything."

"You're welcome, Kendra," I said. Then I stood before each graduate and pretended to move a tassel from one side to the other. "Will you each make a pledge? Will you each promise to perform at least one Seventeen Second Miracle every single day for the rest of your lives?"

They answered silently with three confident nods.

"The watches are now yours."

Back in the car, I turned in the opposite direction we'd come. I followed my mother, plus Kendra and Jade, who'd decided to ride with her even farther from town.

"Where are we going now?" Miles asked.

I let him wonder.

"I don't know," Travis offered. "But can you imagine how nuts Kendra is going right now?"

We laughed again because it felt good to laugh. And we laughed because we knew it was true.

The drive to Laurel Hills was another half hour. We parked next to one another in the visitors' parking lot and stretched our legs.

Miles helped Travis into his chair.

"As often as I can I come here to visit someone. I thought you might like to come, too, and you can consider it part of your final exam."

"But you already graduated us," Travis said. "What's up with that?"

I reached down and put his imaginary tassel back to the other side. "Not anymore, champ. Now let's go perform a Seventeen Second Miracle."

We walked into the lobby and were greeted by the nurses at the receptionist's desk. "Another group of grads?" one of them asked.

"Sure are."

"Congratulations," she said. "And he's in a good mood today, Cole. Have fun."

I led Mom, Jade, and the kids down a long white hallway to the very last room. I smiled when I looked at some of the rooms we passed, many of which were empty.

With each step closer I tried to remember exactly when I decided that my dad wasn't wasting his time.

I could hear his voice in my head: *Love is a verb, boy. Seventeen seconds to thank her for dinner. Seventeen seconds to buy a bouquet on the way out of the grocery store. You can save your marriage, a life, a friendship, just seventeen seconds at a time.*

I've been to this facility many times and, I hope, brightened many faces. But yesterday I visited only my favorite. He has Alzheimer's disease. It began much earlier than it should have and took his mind much faster than doctors were prepared for. The reality today is that every seventeen seconds I spend with him are new.

I pushed open the door and held it for the others. "Hi, there."

He was sitting by the window reading a magazine he wouldn't remember in the morning. A pocket watch rested on his lap. "My goodness, my goodness, my, my. What a lovely group. What are your names?"

It still hurts that I have to introduce myself every time, but I do it because I know it's the only way.

"My name is Cole."

The others introduced themselves, too, even Jade and my mother.

When they'd finished, I invited Travis forward. "And this one, this one is going to be living with us."

"He is?" His enthusiasm lifted me.

"That's right. We're building a brand-new ramp just so he can get onto our porch."

"You have a porch? I love porches."

"So do I. Actually, I think we all do, right, gang?"

Nods and smiles.

"Well, my, my, I am just so glad you've come. Would you like to see my favorite pocket watch? I have a collection."

I took it from his hand, admired it just as I had many times before, and passed it around the room.

As Jade gingerly returned the watch to his outstretched palms I asked, "Would you mind if we told you a story?"

"Of course, I adore stories."

With the help of everyone in the room, we retold the story of the original Seventeen Second Miracle, a story from 1970, the moment a young girl named Lisa Ann, or Flick, left this life at her own birthday party.

He watched every word leave our mouths with rapt attention to every colorful detail. From the day of the week to the name of the lake, from the name of Flick's mother to the pile of unopened presents on the picnic table.

He wept openly as I concluded and I did what I always do. I put my arms around him and said, "It's OK."

When he'd gathered himself, which took as much time as it always did, he looked at each of us and said, "It wasn't his fault, was it?"

"No," my mother answered. "It wasn't."

"Did it lead to something to good?" he asked, still wiping his nose with a handkerchief.

"It did," my mother answered. "It led to *this*." She held her hands out proudly as if we were some prize to be won, a reward for a lifetime of service.

The corners of his mouth turned down again. "I hope he wasn't too hard on himself through all those years. All that guilt he must have felt. But it could have happened to anybody, right?"

"That's right," Jade said, looking not at him, but at Travis. "It could have happened to anyone."

Travis looked up, hardly an inch of dry skin on his young face.

After the moment passed, I looked at our host again and asked him to stand. "You look mighty spiffy in that outfit. I bet you can't keep the ladies off you."

Mother laughed.

"Thank you, my boy, you just made my day."

"Well, it's only fair," I answered. "Because you made my life, Dad."

He took a moment to survey the faces in the room. "You're my son."

It came as half-question, half-recognition.

"I am."

He took another pause. "And why did you come?"

"Because you're our Seventeen Second Miracle."

"Oh," he said. "How wonderful. Well, my boy, you know what I heard once?"

"What's that?"

"Love is a verb."

The Seventeen Second Miracle

1. Why do you think most people blame Rex for Flick's drowning? Do you think that is a fair assessment? Why or why not?

2. Losing a child is an emotional hardship. Do you think Flick's mother was so unforgiving of Rex because she thought he could have prevented Flick's death, or is there something more to her ire?

3. Forgiveness can be a slow process. Discuss why Sparks and Rex stay together even after everything that's happened in their relationship, and to her family. Did you ever doubt they would be able to make their relationship work?

4. Why do you think Sparks was so quick to forgive Rex and help him heal?

5. Discuss the significance of Cole and Jade's porch and how it becomes a point of contention when Jade considers it *Cole's* porch, but also how it becomes a haven for them and others.

6. Jade and Cole cannot have children and Jade has come to feel defeated by God. At one point, Jade says, "I won't feel sorry for myself and blame God. I won't. I'll just live a different life from the one I dreamt of" (page 121). Discuss how this tests their faith and marriage.

7. Rex "knew no strangers" (page 136). How does this work in context with his life's work in performing, witnessing, and collecting Seventeen Second Miracles?

8. Jade gives Cole braids that symbolize the past, present, and future, and encourages him to remember what the Discussions are really about. Why do you think it took so long for Jade to have this conversation with him? How do you think it changed how Cole led the Discussions from then on?

9. Would you consider the incident with Travis on the mall a failed miracle? Why or why not? Are there other examples throughout the novel where the characters are confronted with a failed miracle, only to have their faith see them through?

10. At the end of chapter 31, Cole says, "I retrieved Travis's watch. It worked, but it was badly beaten" (page 161). How is this symbolic of what just happened in the story? Were Travis's actions toward Cole justified after the incident?

11. Why do you think Jade is willing to give up Paper Gems if they can't arrest the arsonist? How does this exemplify the type of person she is?

12. As an apology to Jade, Cole buys three dozen roses and tucks a card into each vase, telling her to open them in any order. Discuss the symbolism and significance of the order in which she opens them: "You. I. Love" (page 219).

13. Cole and Jade fight on their honeymoon because Cole is performing a miracle after Jade asks him not to get involved. Is it ever possible for a miracle to be detrimental?

14. At one point, Cole contemplates that his father raised him in Seventeen Second Miracles. Do you think there is any truth to this?

15. Do you think that Cole was better prepared for the Discussions by not following in his father's footsteps? Why or why not?

16. Discuss the difference between "being good" and being a "goody-goody" (page 238) in the context of the story and Rex's life.

17. Have you ever performed or experienced a Seventeen Second Miracle?

The Seventeen Second
Miracle Challenge

Here is a place to record the miracles you perform for others and those performed for you. When these pages are full, create your own Seventeen Second Miracle journal.

_____

_____

_____

_____

_____

_____

_____

_____